THE VANISHED: AN AUDREY LORD MYSTERY

G C CHASE

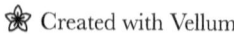

1

Darkness. Silence. Sally's head pounded as she woke. Why was she sitting with her knees up? Her lower back ached. Where was she? She stretched out her hands. Wood.

On either side of her. In front. Above her. A box or crate. Stretching out her arms, she followed the contour of the wood. It curved. Like a barrel. Her heart raced and her breath became quick and shallow.

Why was she in a barrel? And what had happened to her date? She called out for help. Her voice was a whisper, dry, muffled by the walls. The sound echoed around her, but no one responded. She was alone. Had her date done this?

Tears rolled down her cheeks as she replayed the night. Him sitting opposite her, her trying not to grin at how handsome he was. Everything was perfect. The restaurant. How he was already at the table waiting for her, unlike others.

He knew about wine and ordered a local Pinot, and when they ordered and settled into the night, how easily the conversation flowed. He talked about his work in IT. She talked about her job in sales. But then what?

He asked for the bill. She offered to pay half, but he waved her away. He said something she liked. She remembered now. *You can get the next one if it bothers you. Next time.* She liked that.

He was different from the others. Even the way he paid cash with crisp notes from his wallet. Most people paid by card. The waiter looked happy, so it must have been a good tip. She was generous and liked that in others. Then they left.

Outside, the air was mild. Summer was on its way. She'd felt light, giddy. It was hard to tell if it was because of the glass of wine she finished or that the night was going so well. She had a good feeling about this one. A group of girls in their teens wearing luminous short dresses bustled past them, huddled together, arms linked, swaying like they had been drinking.

They passed the police station and came to the Esplanade. His arm linked in hers as they discussed which way to go. The options were to go straight ahead to Schnapper Point Road and then down to the pier and yacht club, or cross the road and walk along Mother's Beach and Shire Hall Beach until the foreshore reserve prevented them from going any farther.

The beach was well populated at night with couples looking for privacy and kids smoking vapes and sipping cruisers in the shadows away from prying parental eyes. But she let him pick which way to walk. Why? All because he paid for dinner? She felt a pang of regret.

They turned right and walked along the Esplanade, past a mix of original, restored weatherboards and newer mansions with uninterrupted views out across the bay, picking out the ones they liked. Halfway along she stopped at number 820, a neo-Tudor style clinker brick and shingle-tiled house that most locals knew.

Its name was Combe Martin, and it was one of Mornington's best-known homes. He didn't know the place but could see the appeal. The last time it came up for sale, she went to the open house with her friend Anna. The estate agent frowned as they walked in, so Anna grabbed her hand like they were a couple.

He laughed, enjoying the story, so she continued telling him about the refined elegance of English workmanship and seven hundred square metres of luxury living, and how away from the agent's suspicious glare they had hurried around the property like excited children. Imagining themselves sipping drinks with their respective loved ones in the mahogany library, throwing fabulous dinner parties in the dining room with its French doors, and enjoying family time in the spacious kitchen with a butler's pantry.

Did she bore him?

The old Sally would tell him how the master bedroom had captured her heart with its fitted walk-in robe, sumptuous en suite and panoramic views of the bay. How she imagined herself lying there with her significant other. Or that she knew she would never own a home like that, no matter how much she saved.

She didn't belong in a house like that. The house would always know she was a visitor who would only stay until its proper owner turned up. And that every time she passed the property, she felt both awe and loathing at the promise of what could never be. The new Sally knew not to say things like that.

New Sally also didn't tell him that as she stood in that bedroom, she felt how much she wanted a family and someone to love. How she knew time was running out. How she often caught herself watching her elderly parents with renewed interest. How one remembered the half of the story the other one forgot. How they put sunscreen on each other's back.

She wanted a different version, of course. All kids did. New Sally knew not to go into any of that. She'd made that mistake before. Sharing too early. Telling things like they were. But then would come the signs. The glancing at other tables. Checking the watch. The realisation she'd blown it again.

Not this time. This one was different. Maybe even *the one?* Which was why when his hand slipped into hers like they had been together much longer than three hours, she stole a furtive glance and agreed to what came next.

Gesturing to the right, he asked, "Is Mills Beach along there?"

Yes. She knew it was deserted at night. He told her a story about how his father only ever took them to the beach twice, and once was to Mills Beach. She felt sorry for him. Then he asked about the hill.

The one that Sally and her friends struggled up after a day at the beach. She told him how Anna and Di would run ahead while Sally panted her way to the top, which was why she had joined a gym and got fit.

She didn't tell him that at fifty-eight kilograms, she could now bench press a hundred, run thirty minutes, and couldn't remember the last time she did less than fifteen thousand steps a day. How following clients around liquor stores to get their order helped and that Mills Beach was no match for her now.

She didn't want to brag.

He asked if they could go. She knew better than to follow a stranger, even a cute one, down to a dark beach. But instead of saying no, she checked her phone to make sure it had enough charge. Why did she do that? Pathetic.

They walked to the beach, but then what? Why couldn't she remember? Was she drugged? Did he slip something into her drink when she went to the bathroom? Drugs could cause a person to lose hours.

A chilling thought circled. Was that why he gave the waiter a large tip? Did the waiter see something? Was it his way to placate him? But if he meant to hurt her… why a barrel? It made no sense. That was the worst part.

There were barrels at work. She'd been in one before. After the new bar opened, someone had suggested they see who could fit. Sally, Gavin, and the new girl in accounts were the only ones small enough to squeeze in.

She had felt claustrophobic and wanted to get out, but Lucas asked her about the smell. He said each wooden barrel had its own unique scent that reminded him of a campfire with a hint of sawdust.

Everyone laughed, but unperturbed, he kept saying how much he loved the earthy, smoky, and warm scent that brought out the nuances of the drink inside. Was that where she was now? At work? Had she taken her date to the brewery? The bar might have been open, but then what?

Her mouth was dry, like a normal morning. Was it Saturday morning? The brewery was open on Saturdays. But it was too quiet. Trucks and the forklift would be moving around. She sniffed. All the brewery's barrels had a scent. Nothing. So, if she wasn't at work, where was she?

2

S unday

Audrey Lord climbed the stairs towards the only rooftop bar in Bennington, feeling apprehensive. The bayside town that sat between Melbourne and the gateway to the Mornington Peninsula polarised people.

Outsiders preferred to lock their car doors and keep driving farther down the Mornington Peninsula to Rye or Portsea, while locals boasted about proximity to the beach and bay for half the price you paid in the city. They overlooked the drugs, crime, and occasional serial killer, considering it a small price to pay.

Audrey grew up in Bennington and knew the area, having spent many nights here in her youth, but she would always ask someone to walk her back to the car. But it wasn't the area's reputation making her feel uneasy. Most social occasions came with a sense of trepidation. She had avoided the last two school reunions, using kids and work as an excuse, but there was no getting out of this one.

Victoria Renshaw, the reunion organiser—perfect manicure, Gucci handbag, genuine tan—had cornered her at parent-teacher interviews insisting they connect on Facebook and swap mobile numbers. Facebook was easy: connect and then unfollow, but sharing phone numbers felt like a bigger surrender.

When it became clear Victoria wasn't backing down, Audrey had accepted the invitation. On some level, she knew it would do her good to get out and mix with adults. Since Mark had taken a job on the rig, she didn't do it enough—but didn't have to like it.

She climbed the stairs and walked onto the timber deck. The place had been renovated since her last visit. A timber wall ran along the left-hand side to waist height with a glass screen above it so customers could enjoy the view. On the opposite side of the highway was the hotel and beyond that the beach and bay, visible even though the light was fading. The spring air was clear and mild. It was the perfect night for a reunion.

Small tables were dotted along the outside walls, but the fifty or so in attendance stood in the middle, talking in groups. You could tell the ones who wanted to be here. They grinned and laughed, while the reticent ones gripped their drinks tightly and nodded.

A table with handwritten stickers was positioned near the entry. A quick count revealed there were about twenty to show, including Cath Maguire, Audrey's friend and lead detective at Bennington Police.

Audrey smiled. She knew Cath wasn't keen, but the persistent Victoria had gotten to her as well. Audrey found her name tag and pasted it onto her emerald-green midi dress. Only nineteen to go now. Facing the room, she gulped. Where to start? She walked over to the bar and read the wine list.

"A glass of the Dromana sparkling, thanks."

The barman, who looked to be in his forties, smiled. "Coming right up."

His upbeat manner put her at ease. She hadn't planned to return to her hometown, but journalist jobs were thin on the ground, so here she was. She paid for her drink and took a sip. Maybe this wouldn't be so bad after all.

Audrey was working out who to speak with when she saw Victoria Renshaw with two women. Victoria caught her eye and gestured for her to join them.

"I'm so glad you came," said Victoria, drawing Audrey in for a kiss on the cheek. Victoria's face was flushed from alcohol or excitement or both.

"Stella, Leonie, this is Audrey."

Audrey smiled at the two women. She recognised Stella, a bookish woman with enormous freckles. "We were in biology together, weren't we?"

"That's right. I had to sit up front because I couldn't hear the teacher. I'm a researcher now with the Commonwealth Scientific and Industrial Research Organisation."

Leonie was a tall woman with a horsey face and enormous, kind brown eyes. Audrey couldn't place her, which must have showed.

"I only came in year nine," said Leonie. "What are you doing with yourself?"

Victoria's eyes widened. "Audrey is a reporter at the *Gazette*."

Despite Victoria's enthusiasm, it grated hearing it out loud that she worked for the local newspaper instead of one of the major newspapers. Her usual explanation was that her husband Mark worked on a rig half the time, and the hours suited life with the kids, but justifying why she wasn't where she wanted to be professionally was annoying. How long was she going to keep blaming Mark and the kids?

To her relief, Victoria changed tack. "Audrey's daughter Beth and mine go to school together."

Leonie and Stella smiled politely. Audrey and Mark could never have afforded the fees, but Beth was a sporty student who realised this early and took it upon herself to secure a scholarship. "Beth got herself a scholarship. Her twin brother goes to the high school."

One more thing her twins didn't have in common. Despite Audrey's best efforts, the only thing her two children seemed to share was their birth. Audrey and Mark both hoped that would change before one of them—most likely Beth—left home to explore the world.

"Don't get me started on teenagers," said Stella.

Victoria brightened. "Oh look, there's Rebecca. Do excuse me, ladies. I'll leave you to catch up." She sashayed away to greet more guests.

Leonie kept the conversation going. "My daughter is so moody, and my son ignores everything I say and has taken up vaping because everyone does it."

Stella stepped in. "I showed my daughter a paper on the toxins in those things, thinking it would change her mind, but she wasn't interested. She only stopped when a friend said it ruined her skin. I don't know if that's true, but it worked."

Eventually, it was time to circulate, and so they agreed to stay in touch via the Facebook group. Decision time. Should she move to water so she could leave soon or enjoy another glass of bubbles and bunk in for another hour before it was safe to drive? The kids didn't care, so there was no hurry. She walked over to the barman.

"Another glass of the Dromana sparkling, thanks."

As she waited for her drink, a large man she didn't recognise with ruddy skin, wearing a business shirt and chinos, was at the table putting on a nametag. Craig. She vaguely remembered him being good at football. Victoria welcomed him, but after a brief chat the smile she had worn all night vanished. Something was wrong.

Victoria looked over and gestured for Audrey to join them. She paid for her drink and made her way over.

"Audrey works for the *Gazette*. She might be able to help."

"Is everything okay?"

Craig spoke. "Hi Audrey. A friend of mine, Sally Child, has gone missing."

Audrey scanned the Filofax of names from school but came up short. "I don't remember the name."

"She was a couple of years below us." Craig showed them a photo of Sally—a healthy-looking woman in her thirties, light brown silky hair, wearing gym pants and a singlet with the beach behind her.

"How long has she been missing?"

"She went out for dinner last night on Main Street, Mornington with a date and hasn't been seen since. Her phone goes straight to voicemail. Car's still in the carpark near the supermarket."

Was Sally with her date? Plenty of people went off the grid for a weekend after a date that went well. "Any chance she's lying low for a day or two?"

Craig shook his head. "Not Sally. Every day without fail she takes her parents coffee in the retirement village. Never missed a day since they moved in. She also goes for a walk every morning at Bennington Beach and posts a photo on Facebook. Got a pretty big following on Insta, and nada there too."

Audrey could hear the panic in his voice. "Have you been able to contact her date?"

Craig's voice rose. "Nobody knows who he is. Not even her bestie, Di. We've tried to contact him via her Insta page, but there's been no response. They didn't book at the restaurant, so there's no record of him there either."

Sally's date might not have seen the post, and plenty of places on Main Street took walk-ins, but it was unusual that her best friend didn't know who he was.

"We've notified the police. I'm not sure what else we can do."

Did Cath know about Sally? Was that why she wasn't here?

Audrey was keen to help. "I think the best way I can help is by writing a piece on Sally so people know she's missing. We can post online and on the paper's social media page."

Craig nodded eagerly. "That'd be great. I'll send you a photo."

Victoria's work was done here. "I'll leave you both to it then. I hope your friend turns up." She patted Craig's arm and left to continue her hosting duties.

While Craig chose an image, Audrey brought up Cath's number and sent a text. *Are you working on Sally Child?*

The response was quick. *No flies on you. Looking into it.*

Cath was a good detective, so Sally was in excellent hands.

Dogs sense storms. Journalists, stories. Twenty-four hours off the grid appeared to be a big deal for Sally, which meant something was wrong.

3

———————

Bennington was blessed, or cursed, with a pub on all four corners of the main intersection. On warm nights, the crowd at Bennington Pub spilled out onto the deck of the beachside establishment to take in the sunset.

A late-afternoon breeze had forced everyone inside, so it was noisier than usual, but it didn't bother him. The opposite, in fact. After all, he was celebrating.

Sally Child was no longer a problem.

He'd watched her for weeks, learning her patterns. Same route to work, same coffee shop, same evening jog. She'd made it so easy, creatures of habit always did. The fact that he couldn't tell anyone didn't matter. His insides felt electric.

He bought a drink and stood to the side. The mood was upbeat. A group of young guys were chatting up two young girls. One girl was falling for their charms, judging by the way she grinned and leaned in. The other one clocked him and smiled. He was old enough to be her father, but it felt good to know he still had it. He only ever wanted sex at their place, never his, and then to leave.

Sipping his beer, he spotted a group of women in their forties in a booth. The one in the middle dabbed at her eyes while her friends comforted her. A divorce, maybe? Later, when she hit the anger stage, her friends would tell her to forget the bastard. He'd made that mistake before and had no intention of listening to stories of an ex who fooled around for hours. At the bar, two guys in their thirties were doing shots. That was more like it.

He approached the two men. "What are we drinking, fellas?"

The two guys looked curious. Why was a guy asking them this? But once they saw him, any doubts disappeared. It had always been that way. His mother and her friends told him what a good-looking boy he was. His father was proud of his boy sowing his wild oats and being able to take his pick. Hell, at one point, someone even suggested he consider modelling. His rugged looks and blue eyes and full head of hair could sell yachts and sailing boats or outdoor equipment. He'd make a fortune. Why didn't he? Because all he wanted was to be left alone.

"Tequila, man." The guy with shaggy blonde hair's eyes sparkled from the booze.

"Three shots of tequila." The barman filled three shot glasses in front of them.

The other one, dark-haired, Italian-looking, picked up his drink. "Salute."

"Salute." They all downed the drinks.

He paid cash.

Shaggy hair spoke. "Thanks, man. You from around here?"

"Up north. Got sick of the humidity and biblical rain, so when I was looking for options, the Peninsula came out on top."

It was the Italian one's turn. "How long have you been down here?"

"Couple of years now."

As the alcohol buzzed around his system, he enjoyed the company and innocuous questions.

It was shaggy hair's turn again. "You work out, mate?"

He prickled at the memory. "I get to the gym when I can."

"Which gym?" said shaggy hair.

It was one question too many. "Sorry, fellas. I've got to be somewhere."

Of course he did. A guy like him had to have things on. The two men shook his hand.

He headed out into the cool air. On the way to his car, a cop car cruised past. He was over the limit and screwed if he lost his licence. Pivoting, he walked across the bridge towards the beach. He stepped onto the sand and took a deep breath.

The cool night air filled his lungs. A rush of anxiety tasted bitter, like mouldy bread. What was he worried about? There was no way of tying him to her disappearance. No one saw them. There was no CCTV and definitely none where he had taken her. The way he organised everything was masterful.

A wave subsided and with it his worry. He stared towards the black bay and smiled.

4

Audrey arrived home to find Josh in the kitchen, pouring hot water over pot noodles. The late-night snacks had started six months ago. It seemed like the only time he wasn't eating was when he was asleep.

"Still hungry?" Audrey kissed him on the cheek. Were those whiskers? The sweet boy who used to smell like biscuits was turning into a man more and more each day.

"Starving."

Audrey propped herself at the kitchen table and took out her laptop. As she waited for it to whir to life, she opened Facebook. On the way home, she'd spoken to her colleague Donna, who managed the newspaper's social media, about Sally. The post about the missing woman was up already. Good.

Josh slurped Kewpie mayonnaise over his noodles and, to Audrey's pleasant surprise, didn't head to his room but sat opposite her.

"You working?"

Any questions about the reunion—who came, who wore what, what was everybody doing now—would come from Josh's twin, Beth. Josh was more concerned with the here and now. In this case, why his mother was working so late.

"A woman's gone missing, and I'm posting details online in case anyone has seen her or knows anything."

Josh looked down, mouth full, and chewed. To anyone else, it would be difficult to tell which, if any, parts of that statement had registered. In the company of his quick-talking sister, he sometimes appeared slow. But Audrey and Mark knew their son took time to process and then formulate questions.

"Why do people think she's missing?"

Audrey smiled. It was a good question. "Because they haven't been able to contact her for twenty-four hours, which is very out of character."

"What's out of character?" Beth walked in wearing pyjama pants and a hoodie. Even at this hour, there was an intensity to her speech and movements. She'd also need more context than Josh.

"A woman has gone missing. She went out for dinner last night with a date no one knows and hasn't been seen since. Her car is still in the car park."

Beth sat at the head of the table and frowned at Josh's noodles. She refused to let anything comprising preservatives, chemicals, inflammatory oils, or any other unknown ingredients pass her lips.

"She could be with her date."

It had only been twenty-four hours, and that was a real possibility.

"Maybe, but her friends don't think so. She normally visits her parents every day."

Beth looked surprised. "Every day?"

Audrey stifled a grin. She didn't expect her own children to visit that often in her dotage, which was just as well, going by the look on Beth's face.

"And she posts on social media every day. Her phone's been off since Friday night. She's got a decent following too, so going silent seems odd."

That landed. Going offline was a whole different issue for Beth.

"What's her name?"

"Sally Child."

Beth tapped the keys on her phone and turned the screen to show an image of Sally Child on Instagram.

Audrey leaned in. "That's her."

As Beth scrolled through the page, Audrey began her article.

Sally Child went out for dinner last night in Mornington with a date and hasn't been seen since.

Beth stopped scrolling. "That's really weird."

"What is?" Audrey paused her typing.

"Her engagement is okay during the week, but it's huge on weekends."

Audrey looked at her daughter. "Meaning?"

"You don't not post on the day that gets the biggest likes. Something must be wrong."

Social media had become a vital tool in missing persons cases. But was a person's posting behaviour now a predictor of whether something was truly wrong?

"Even if things went well with her date? If she had bigger things going on?"

Beth had yet to start dating, but Audrey suspected it was imminent. Whispered conversations to friends. Boys' names dropped here and there. Beth guarded her phone like a diary, and lately, even more so.

"You'd find the time, Mum. It takes like a minute to post."

Josh looked at his sister. In no universe would he ever openly agree. One day, maybe, but not yet. Audrey could tell he did, though.

Audrey continued typing. *Her friends and family are concerned for her safety.*

Josh sat back for a break. "Maybe she went down to the beach, and he got her there. Pretty stupid if she did."

Beth snapped. "What if she did? Are you victim-blaming?"

Josh wisely took another mouthful of noodles. It wasn't clear if he understood what that meant, but he knew enough about his sister to know it wasn't good. "No."

Beth didn't believe him. "We talked about this in Ms Pental's class."

Ms Pental was a new and popular teacher at Beth's school who liked to encourage lively discussions in history class.

"Next you'll be asking why she was out after dark and what she was wearing. It shifts the responsibility for safety in public away from the perpetrators of crimes and onto women and girls. Women should be able to go out in public after dark and be safe. Mum?"

Violence against women in Australia is all too common. Audrey had read the statistics. Approximately one in three women over fifteen had experienced physical assault, one in five sexual assault, and over half at least one incident of physical or sexual violence in their lifetime. The national strategy promoted equal and respectful relationships between men and women at all levels of society. She was doing her bit—raising a kind, respectful son, albeit one with dribbles down his chin, but it was no easy fix.

"Of course I agree, but the reality can be different."

Beth stood. "Well, change has to start somewhere. I'm not going to live my life in fear. I hope she turns up safely."

Beth's courage was admirable, if naïve. Audrey also worried it meant she wouldn't be as cautious as she should be.

"Night. I hope so too."

Audrey typed the final line. *If you have any information about Sally Child's whereabouts, contact Mornington Police.*

She hit post. Hopefully by morning, Sally would turn up safely—perhaps even a little embarrassed her disappearance had caused concern.

5

The following morning, there was no sign of Sally. It had now been thirty-six hours.

Audrey drove towards Mornington, Sally's last known whereabouts, to join Craig and a group of friends searching the beaches at the bottom of Main Street. Concern had turned to panic. A second search was already underway at Bennington Beach.

The first forty-eight hours were crucial. Each one that passed made it less likely a missing person would be found. The best way Audrey could help was by keeping Sally's name in the news — and for that, she needed to know more about her.

She turned off the highway into Beleura Hill Road and followed it down to the Esplanade. The road was quiet. Mills Beach was the first of the small coves, a pretty, private spot during the day, at night it was dark and deserted. A thick clump of scrub separated it from the more populated Shire Hall Beach and Mothers Beach. The perfect hiding spot for a body?

It was a curse of the profession to think the worst.

Audrey parked on the beach side of the Esplanade near Mothers Beach and spotted Craig talking to an elderly couple. As she climbed out, he saw her, excused himself, and hurried across the sand.

"Thanks for coming. It's all hands on deck today."

"No problem."

Craig was a talker. Audrey waited, giving him space to fill in any new information.

"People are looking for Sal's wallet or keys, in case she dropped them. We're thinking that because it was a nice night, they might have come down to the beach for a walk."

Half a dozen adults were combing the sand. Audrey scanned the scrub. Was anyone searching over there? Or at Mills Beach? Or at Sally's home?

She had to ask. "Is someone keeping an eye on her place?"

Craig nodded quickly. "Her folks checked again today. Sal's house is always tidy — it's hard to tell if she's been there. But nothing looks out of place. They're pretty sure she hasn't been back."

"Her car? Still in the car park?"

"Yep. Locked. No sign of her handbag or anything inside."

That wasn't good. Sally could have left it voluntarily — but for two days?

A man in his thirties called out from the beach. "Nugget! We're heading round to Mills!"

Nugget, huh? With his ruddy complexion and solid build, it fit.

"Sal's no fool. She'd know better than to go there at night," Craig muttered, but acknowledged the man with a nod.

He rubbed his forehead. Hands shaking. Panic rising.

Audrey offered an escape. "Can you show me where she had dinner? Maybe tell me more about her? The more I know, the easier it'll be to keep our readers thinking about her."

Craig brightened slightly. "Sure."

They crossed the road and walked up Main Street, past the police station and closed-up restaurants, some were being cleaned. A few minutes of silence seemed to calm him.

"Some mates have little sisters who flirt or annoy you to get attention. Not Sal. She used to bring us snacks while we were mid-game on Xbox. Took their stupid dog for long walks so it didn't wake us after a big night. She was just... really kind."

It was hard to imagine Beth bringing Josh snacks during Xbox.

"She also takes her folks coffee every morning after her beach walk."

Audrey felt a quiet pang. When was the last time she brought her parents anything other than grandchildren?

Craig clearly cared for Sally. Knew a lot about her movements. Audrey looked for a ring. No sign of one.

"And no, I don't have a thing for her," he added, as if reading her thoughts. "Everyone knows her routine because she tells us all the time. Bed by nine. Walking six to six-thirty. Coffee with her folks. Gym Monday, Tuesday, Thursday, and once on the weekend. Christ, I know her schedule better than my ex-wife's. But that's a whole other story."

So maybe he did have feelings for her.

They stopped at a closed Italian restaurant.

"This is where they had dinner. She posted this Thursday night, eight-ten."

He showed Audrey a photo of seafood linguine on his phone.

"The waiter remembered she was with a guy. Paid cash. Gave a good tip. Brown hair. Six foot. Good-looking."

The police might have more luck with the description. But paying cash wasn't typical.

"Any idea how she met him?"

Craig flinched. "Not really. Rick said she was on eHarmony, so maybe there."

Audrey nodded. Donna was on Match — more for hookups, though it could lead to something. eHarmony was for people looking long-term. Sally had wanted something serious.

"You don't think it's a good idea?" Audrey asked.

"I get it. Everyone's married. But meeting a perfect stranger like that freaks me out. I'm old-school."

Audrey couldn't argue. The statistics around dating apps were disturbing. One in ten sex offenders reportedly used them. A quarter of rapists. Thousands of abductions and murders each year linked to online predators. But there were success stories too of happy marriages, and lifelong friendships.

Still, it was hard not to worry. Her own kids would likely use dating apps one day. She pushed the thought away.

"This area would've been busy Friday night," she said. "Maybe someone took a selfie. Might have caught her in the background."

"Is Sally's best friend here today?" Audrey couldn't remember her name.

Craig shook his head. "Di's in Cairns seeing her folks. Couldn't get a flight out till tomorrow. First holiday in five years, but she insisted on cutting it short. They're close."

And yet Di didn't know who Sally's date was?

Craig's phone buzzed. "Sorry. Got to take this."

As he turned away, Audrey's phone buzzed too. Beth.

Where are you?

She replied: *At a search for the missing woman. Be home later.*

Beth had a friend coming to study. Josh wanted to play Xbox. For once, no one needed a lift.

Beth replied with a simple: *OK.*

Despite the cold tone, Audrey added a heart emoji. She didn't expect one back.

Craig returned, face pale.

"They found Sal's jacket in Bennington," he said quietly. "At the park near the footy oval. Some old guy out walking rang the police. They're down there now."

Audrey swallowed. The park was fifteen minutes away.

Craig tried to sound hopeful. "She might've lost it, or had it stolen and they tossed it later, right?"

A wallet maybe. But women didn't lose their jackets.

6

Thirty minutes later, Audrey drove along the highway towards Bennington, only this time with her colleague, trainee journalist Donna, in the passenger seat.

Whip-smart, with long black painted fingernails that demanded attention, Donna was in her mid-twenties. She was going to make a brilliant journalist provided she worked on her tendency to pick a direction too soon and not consider all the facts. Her social media stalking skills were legendary.

Audrey was about to meet the cast and crew from Sally's world and wanted an extra set of eyes and ears to help. Donna wanted as much field experience as she could get.

"How did they know it was her jacket?"

"No idea. There must have been something inside to identify her."

After the call, Craig had hurried off to tell the others the news, but they would find out soon enough.

Donna looked pensive. She used online sites and dated regularly. Was this a little too close to home?

"Are you sure you're okay to come with me today?"

Donna's head recoiled. "Absolutely. A woman should be able to go out on a date and not have anything happen to her."

It had been over a decade since Jill Meagher was stalked, raped, and murdered on her way home in Brunswick. Eurydice Dixon was stalked for over an hour and four kilometres before being murdered in a park. Most women still didn't feel safe, even though they should.

The football oval was on the right and beyond that where Sally's items had been found. The park was a popular spot for wedding photos because of the elm trees and ponds and tiny bridges that couples stood on together. A beautiful day to take wedding photos, except today they would be crime-scene shots of Sally Child's items.

Audrey drove along the perimeter of the park. Up ahead were two police vehicles. An officer was talking to a group of people. Another was directing morning walkers away from the area.

In the distance, two detectives stood with an elderly man. She recognised one as her old school friend, Detective Cath Maguire. Journalists and the police often had a tense relationship but learning that Cath was a senior detective at Bennington was one of the few bright spots in coming back. Audrey was careful never to overstep the mark.

She parked the car.

"How do you want to do this?" Donna asked, surveying the small crowd of onlookers.

Craig was comforting a string bean of a man with shaggy brown hair and an AC/DC t-shirt. Sally's brother Rick? He had all the hallmarks of someone in shock. Face pale and eyes wide. Mouth slightly open like in the midst of saying something, but no words come out. Body rigid and tense, ready to flee at any moment. Craig grabbed the man's shoulder. It worked and calmed him down.

An elderly couple, arms linked, walked towards them. The man was tall and thin and reminded Audrey of a greyhound. The woman was a foot shorter, with a pristine grey bob and pretty face. Rick hugged the woman. His mother, perhaps? Craig shook the elderly man's hands and leaned down to kiss the woman on the cheek.

"The parents?" Donna asked.

"I think so. You take the guys. I'll speak to the parents."

Craig did the introductions. "Bill and Olive. This is Audrey from the Bennington Gazette."

Bill gave her a solemn nod of acknowledgement. The man had

bigger things to worry about than being friendly, but she wanted to establish rapport.

"I was at a school reunion with Craig and wanted to see if I could help. The more people who know you're looking for Sally, the better."

This seemed to placate Bill, who took a deep breath and nodded.

Olive looked at Audrey. "I don't understand how she could go out for dinner in Mornington and then her jacket ends up here. Sally doesn't lose things."

But rather than say anything dismissive to his wife, Bill wrapped his arm around her. It spoke volumes about their relationship.

Olive nestled into the embrace until she spotted Donna's hands. "I like your nails. Look at how lovely they are, Bill."

Donna went with it, but Bill looked tired. Dementia, perhaps? The insidious disease took its toll on more than the sufferer.

Rick placed both hands on his head. "I can't believe this is happening."

Olive stepped forward to comfort her son. "It's Sally. She'll be home soon."

But Sally could be anything but fine.

It was time to divide and conquer so Audrey could speak to Sally's parents alone.

Donna took the hint and turned to Craig and Rick. "How about you guys come with me and get coffees?"

In lieu of a better plan, Craig and Rick looked at one another.

"I'll have a latte," said Bill. "And a cappuccino for Olive."

"Back soon." Donna walked off with Craig and Rick.

Audrey turned to Sally's parents. "If it's okay, I'd like to ask you a few things about Sally."

Bill responded. "We've told the police everything we know." But then he winced. "I've got sciatica. A lifetime of sitting at a desk working with PhD students."

Olive smiled. "That's how we met. Bill was a physics lecturer at Monash University, and I was a research fellow."

It was hard not to like Olive.

Audrey spotted a timber bench. "How about we sit over there?"

Bill nodded, so Audrey led them to the bench. Olive sat in the middle and gestured for them to sit on either side of her. Bill groaned with relief as he sat down.

"Surgeon keeps offering me fusion surgery, but I'm too old. But these young ones like to think they can fix everything." He looked at Olive lovingly. "And some things can't be fixed."

Despite his brisk manner, Bill's affection for his wife was endearing.

"Craig was telling me Sally brings you a coffee every morning."

Olive's voice was full of concern. "But she didn't yesterday, did she, Bill?"

Bill took Olive's hand. "No, love. Which is how we knew something was wrong."

Olive said, "She goes to the coffee shop at the Eliza James village where we live. They make very nice coffee."

Audrey had driven past the facility. "That's a nice thing for her to do."

No one knew who Sally's mystery date was, but it was worth checking again. "Sally was out for dinner the night she went missing. Did she mention who she was catching up with?"

Bill shook his head. "We didn't talk about things like that."

"She didn't say anything to me either," said Olive, looking disappointed. Did all mothers hope their daughters confided in them?

"Craig said Sally worked at the brewery and enjoyed her job."

Olive's eyes lit up again. "Oh, she loves it. They're very good to her, and she gets taken to parties and lots of free samples. She brings us new things to try all the time. What was that one with white wine in it, Bill? You loved that."

Bill cleared his throat. "Yes. They brew it in a white wine barrel. Not cheap, mind you, but it's a nice drop. The process of how they make it is quite fascinating."

Audrey circled back to check Bill's response. "So Sally enjoys her job?"

Bill considered his words. "Yes, she does."

Audrey sensed a "but" coming and waited.

"But over the last couple of months, something changed. She didn't want to talk about work as much. I asked her if everything was okay, and she said she was busy and tired, so I let it go. They had a new beer coming out that I was keen to try, but there seems to have been some sort of delay. Come to think of it, it's been weeks since we spoke about anything to do with work."

Was something going on at work? It could be nothing.

"I need a bathroom," said Olive, looking around for one.

Bill stood. "Excuse us."

Bill led Olive to the public toilets across the road at the football oval.

Audrey spotted a grim-faced Cath Maguire approaching the two officers who had arrived. It was the young officer she first met on the case of Aro Chol, the Sudanese teenager found dead on Chilton Hill. His first sniff of a proper investigation. With his shoulders back, chest out, and chin high, he looked more confident, but Cath outranked him, and by the way he nodded at her instructions, she still called the shots. Audrey waited until Cath was alone and followed her to the police car.

"You missed the reunion last night?"

Cath smirked. "I had to work. Not like you to attend those things. How was it?"

"Okay. Sally's friend Craig was at the reunion."

Cath looked curious. "Really? He seems pretty frantic. Wouldn't have thought a school reunion would be top of mind."

It was a reasonable assumption except for how distressed Craig was.

"He called in to show Sally's photo around."

Cath removed a water bottle from the front seat and took a gulp. "That makes more sense. The family and friends seem a pretty close bunch."

Audrey had only just met them but agreed.

Audrey wouldn't have Cath for long and needed details. "Did the person who found Sally's jacket take it in or phone first?"

"Phoned, fortunately."

Good. It meant that if there were any other clues about how Sally's things got to the park, the police had a better chance of finding out what happened.

"An elderly gentleman who walks in the park every day. He read in the *Gazette* about Sally being missing and thought it could have been important. There was an old healthcare card inside one of the pockets. We got lucky."

Audrey felt a brief surge of pride in the newspaper's role thus far.

"Her father said she works at the brewery. Loves it but lately didn't want to talk about the place so much."

She could tell this was new news to Cath. "We've spoken to them. Said she was a good employee. Loves her job. They're hoping she turns up, as she's their best salesperson. We've also been to her gym. Next Level, on the highway. Everyone loved her there, too."

Two police cars turned up, and officers climbed out.

"Have you spoken to the best friend, Di?" asked Audrey.

"Yes, but they didn't speak this week, so she doesn't know who her date was either."

Craig had said the same thing.

Cath took another gulp of water. "Ground search is about to begin."

"I'll leave you to it. Good luck."

Cath left to address the officers and issue instructions.

By the time Audrey walked back to the bench, Donna had returned, and Bill and Olive were sipping their coffees, watching the ground search commence. Craig and Rick stood nearby with friends who'd come down to show their support.

Audrey took her drink and gestured for Donna to move to the side. "Any joy?"

"Nothing we didn't know, but she sounds like a cool chick."

Craig looked over.

Donna lowered her voice. "He's pretty cut up. He has to go to Adelaide tomorrow for some conference."

"Mentioned that to me, too."

"Leaving the scene of the crime?" Donna's eyes widened.

There she was, choosing a side too early again. "Or maybe he has to go to a conference."

Donna gave Audrey her *you're being a party pooper* face.

The ground search was a painstaking process that would take hours. Was waiting the best use of their time? Only if something turned up, but she could always ring Cath for details later. Audrey was more interested in Bill's comment. Why would someone who loved her job suddenly stop talking about it?

"Come on. This is going to take hours."

Donna sounded relieved. "Where are we going?"

"To the brewery."

7

The drive through the main drag of Bennington wasn't pretty. They passed a sex shop and an eclectic mix of business in various states of disrepair, with a shabby newsagent as the centrepiece. Four police officers stood outside the train station, chatting happily, monitoring activities in the area. At night, their numbers would swell to twenty or more.

"I remember after we moved back, Mark caught the train home from the city after a night out drinking with friends. I kept saying Bennington is one of the safest stations in Melbourne, but he wouldn't believe me. Phoned three times on the way home to make sure I was going to be there on time."

"And?"

"He came out of the station and spotted a dozen police officers on duty, so I got to say, told you so."

Donna smiled. "A marriage highlight?"

Audrey gave a wry smile. Mark was back tomorrow from the oil rig. The first few days were the hardest. Exhausted, he slept while Audrey tiptoed around the house, trying not to resent him being back, disrupting her routine.

But a few days later, the house was cleaned and a meal prepared at night, and she realised how much she missed the support, and eventually him.

"It's our anniversary tomorrow. I need to find somewhere to go."

Donna's tone was incredulous. "You've left this to the day before? Good luck finding somewhere open on a Monday."

Audrey swallowed. She pictured him sitting at the table in silence, the kids on their phones, the microwave humming behind them. Not exactly anniversary material. She rubbed the back of her neck. "Last year I forgot until the morning, so this is an improvement."

Donna frowned and took out her phone. "Wow, lucky guy. I think there's a steak place on the highway, but it's usually super busy." She scanned the available bookings. "Nothing available. Want me to keep looking?"

"Thanks anyway, but I'll find somewhere."

Had Donna hit a nerve? She hadn't anticipated Mark leaving to take the job on the rig. They needed the money, and at the time it was the best option. But what she didn't count on was how hard it would be to parent two teenagers on her own.

Or how Mark lately got to enjoy fantastic training opportunities and meeting people from all around the world. How his world was getting bigger while hers stayed the same. Did she resent this? She hoped not.

She brought the conversation back to work. "What did you think of Craig?"

Donna shrugged. "Seems like a nice enough guy. He's been friends with Rick since primary school and has known Sally since she was born, pretty much. Rick didn't say much, though."

"That's not unusual. Lots of people shut down when they're overloaded."

Audrey turned into an industrial area. Up ahead was a sign for Bennington Brewery. The front courtyard was full of patrons enjoying the sunny weather, either under umbrellas or in the full sun. Audrey pulled into a carpark on the opposite side of the road.

Donna showed Audrey a photo from the company's website of a happy couple in their forties. "That's Lucas Gutterson and his wife Trish."

Lucas wore Bermuda shorts and sunglasses while Trish had on a fashionable button dress in a sixties print with high collar. She had intelligent eyes. "He makes the beer, and she runs the business."

"Hopefully they're here and in the mood for a chat."

They walked through the courtyard inside, where a timber bar ran along one wall. To the rear were rows of barrels, adding to the atmosphere. Audrey paid for their drinks and took them to a table with a good view of the entire place. Donna sipped a Riesling aged beer and Audrey a soda. The infused range of gins was tempting, but even if she wasn't driving, she wanted her wits about her.

Donna took another sip. "This is seriously good beer."

It should be for the price. Mark loved craft beer, so maybe she could bring him here? "I might bring Mark here."

"What guy wouldn't love to go to a brewery?"

Audrey gestured to Lucas, who was chatting to a group near the bar who appeared to be lapping up the tidbits of information he was imparting. He pointed to an area where they could purchase the product and walked behind the bar. Trish Gutterson came out of an office and said something to her husband. Their body language was tense. Trish's voice stayed polite, but her arms crossed and her eyes kept drifting back to the bar. Lucas, on the other hand, leaned in slightly once she'd gone.

"Let's see if they're free for a chat."

They walked up to the bar. Lucas and Trish smiled politely at Audrey and Donna, thinking they were customers.

"My name is Audrey, and this is my colleague, Donna. We work for the Bennington Gazette. I wanted to ask you a few questions about Sally."

Trish's smile disappeared. "We've already spoken to the police, and we know someone found Sally's jacket and wallet."

Her tone indicated that was all she had to say on the matter.

"I know that, but the more people who know about Sally's disappearance, the more chance we have of someone coming forward. I have a few questions."

Audrey waited. She wasn't going away yet.

Two guys in their thirties sauntered up the bar, discussing what they would try next.

Trish looked over at a guy in his early twenties who was loading beer into a fridge. "Jake. Can you serve, please?"

She led them to a barrel with four bar stools to the rear of the building.

Donna's eyes were already glazed from the beer. "This is a really great place." Audrey glanced at the label, which said 11%. No wonder.

"What would you like to know?" Trish said, keeping one eye on the bar.

Lucas was quiet. Audrey directed the next question to him. "I believe Sally worked for you as a sales representative."

Trish cleared her throat. "Sally has been with us for almost two years. She's like family. We're only a small team, so this has hit everyone pretty hard."

Despite her short manner, Trish seemed genuinely distraught.

Finally, Lucas spoke. "Especially Gavin. He started working for us about the same time as Sal as a driver. They're kind of best mates."

Audrey wondered whether Cath's team had spoken to Gavin. She was keen to as well. "I don't suppose he's around at present?"

Trish answered. "He doesn't work weekends. I imagine he's out looking for Sally with her family and friends."

Was he at the search? Perhaps standing with someone else?

"Is there any chance I could speak with him?"

Trish shifted in her seat. "I can't give out his number, but if you have a card, we can ask him to call you."

Trish's attention moved to a group of women in their thirties approaching the bar. "Excuse me. Jake!"

Jake was over in the makeshift bottle shop on his phone. He realised he was needed and, putting his phone away, hurried over to serve.

Trish sighed. "Customers like him, but sometimes he needs a prod."

Jake was a good-looking boy with a cute smile, to which the women appeared to be responding, but he needed help. "Sorry, but I'm going to have to help him."

Trish gave Lucas a look that was hard to read before heading to the bar. Was she warning him to be careful?

Lucas noticed Donna was nearly finished with her beer. "I've got a red version if you're interested."

It was hard to tell if he was buying time or genuinely more focused on the beer.

"That one sat me on my ass." Donna laughed and then regrouped. "Thanks, anyway."

Lucas turned back to Audrey. "Sorry, what was the question?"

"How did Sally get along with her customers?"

Lucas smiled. "Sal's customers loved her. I mean, the occasional one got pissed off because she wouldn't give them stock of our special runs, but she doesn't make it, so that's kind of on me and how many barrels I can get. They can be hard to come by. Was going to make my own, but it was all too hard.

"Sal shared the stock around as best she could and didn't mind telling a few of them they couldn't expect preferential treatment if they only ordered a few times a year. Most liked that she was straight-up with them."

But what about the ones that didn't?

"Did anyone ever get upset?"

Lucas hesitated. His jaw tensed, and his eyes flicked briefly to the floor before returning to hers. "No. I don't think so."

"I mean, you can't give someone something you don't have, right? And at the end of the day, it's just beer."

Trish was finishing up with the women and would be back at any moment.

"Sally was on a date the night she went missing?"

Lucas smiled. "She was pretty excited. No secrets around here. Some guy she met online. They'd been talking for a while and met up. We told her to make it somewhere public. Plenty of nutcases out there."

Lucas's smile faded. "I wish we'd got a name, you know?"

"Any chance she would have told Gavin who he was?"

Lucas shook his head. "First thing we asked him, but he didn't have a clue."

"Not even if they were best friends?"

"I think Gav wished they could be more than friends. Sal knew it too and didn't talk about dating around him."

So Gavin had feelings for Sally. That was interesting.

Trish was now serving another group and looked over at Lucas, pointing to a group of guys waiting to purchase product at the bottle shop.

Lucas stood. "Sorry, but I've got to go."

Audrey handed him her card. "Any reason Sally didn't feel that way about Gavin?"

Lucas breathed in. "Gav's a bit of an odd one. Pretty quiet. I think Sal was after someone…" he appeared to be choosing his words carefully, "different."

"I got to go," said Lucas, signalling he was coming.

"Could you ask Gavin to call me, please?"

"Sure." Lucas pocketed the card and headed over to his customers.

Lucas was barely out of earshot when Donna said, "What if Gavin got jealous and did something to her?"

It was possible, but Audrey didn't want to jump the gun. Everyone's a suspect until they're not. "We need to speak to Gavin. Come on."

Audrey beelined for Jake, who was now outside collecting glasses. "Jake?"

Jake looked up. "I want to leave a note for Gavin. Sorry, what's his surname again?"

Audrey took out a notebook and pen from her handbag.

"Cox."

"Great. Thanks. Don't suppose you know where he lives?"

"I know it's in the Boroughs but couldn't tell you where. If you want to give me the note, I'll make sure it gets to him."

"On second thoughts, I'll call back. What time do the drivers finish each day?"

"About four."

"Thanks for your help."

As they left the brewery, Donna said. "Nice move. Except we don't have an address."

"I know. One step at a time."

Donna checked the time. "So what's next? I'm good for another hour."

The police would be searching the park and they had to wait to speak to Gavin. "Sally spent a lot of time at the gym. Next Level on the highway. It's not far from here. I can drop you off on the way home."

8

Audrey and Donna walked into the reception area of Next Level Fitness. The operators had bought a double-page spread in the *Gazette* when it opened, promising the latest sporting equipment, instructors, and bay views.

It wasn't a place for slouches or the unfit, and members had already managed a degree of fitness and wanted to take it to the next level, hence the name.

The view out to the bay was spectacular, a row of running and cycling machines positioned along the front window to capture it. Behind were rows of gym equipment being used by fit-looking men, for the most part, of various ages.

Donna looked impressed. "A business that actually lives up to its advertising. I should ditch Match and join here."

Weights clanged as they were released. The air was a mix of vanilla and sweat. It had been a long time since Audrey had seen the inside of a gym, but some of the equipment was familiar. The rowing machine. Pull-down. Dumbbells.

These days she preferred walking or jogging around the streets near home.

The front desk was manned by a guy in his mid-twenties with

tanned, dewy skin. He looked up, glowing with good health, and smiled.

"Audrey and Donna from the *Gazette*. I'd like to speak with the manager please."

He headed into the back office, returning with a man in his mid-thirties who also glowed with good health and optimism.

His nametag said Ash. "Ladies. How can I help you?"

Audrey took the lead. "I'm here about one of your members, Sally Child, who I presume you know is missing."

Ash's smile faded. "We're all pretty upset. I take it they haven't found her?"

"Not yet. We ran a brief piece last night, but if we can keep Sally's name out there, someone is more likely to remember something. The first forty-eight hours of a missing persons case is the most critical."

Ash understood the seriousness of the situation but was hesitant. "Do you know Sally?"

Audrey answered. "We haven't met, but I know her parents."

Ash didn't need to know she had just met them.

"I wanted to ask you a few questions if that's okay?" The other man busied himself but was clearly listening. "In private."

Ash led them to an unoccupied corner of the gym. A few members looked up, wondering why two fully clothed women were with the manager, but then went back to their workouts.

Audrey turned to Ash. "I believe Sally spent a lot of time here. I was hoping you might be able to tell me about her life here at the gym. Did she get along with the other members? What she was like?"

Ash took a deep breath. "Sally was, sorry is, a regular. Comes in four times a week. She's a nice lady. Smiles, chats to the other members. I don't know what else I can tell you. We had a Christmas party, which she came to. Got on well with everybody. As far as I can tell, she was happy, but hey, you never know what's going on in some-one's world. I told the police all this."

A loud clang and groan as a set of weights was returned to a bench press made them all look at a red-faced member in his fifties overdoing it.

Donna spoke this time. "Did Sally have any friends here? Anyone she hung out with?"

"There were a couple of people she spoke to a bit." Ash scanned the room. "But none of them are here at the moment."

Donna continued. "Sally was on a date when she went missing. Apparently, it was someone she met online, but is there any chance they met up here?"

Ash shrugged. "I wouldn't know. Like I said, she talks to everyone. It's kind of hard for me to track what goes on outside of here, if you know what I mean."

Suddenly, Ash was on high alert. "Jeff! Wait!"

Jeff, the red-faced member, was about to lift the weights again, but the urgency in Ash's voice made him stop. "The guy's going to kill himself."

Ash signalled to the man that he'd be there in a minute.

This was going nowhere fast.

"What equipment did Sally use?" said Audrey.

Ash looked out across the floor. "The running machine and the rowing machine, although she only started rowing a few months ago."

The rowing machines were off to the side, but the running machines looked out over the bay and beach. Had someone seen Sally from the beach?

"Why do you want to know that?"

"I'm trying to get a feel for how she spent her time while she was here."

Ash glanced over at Jeff. "Sorry. I have to go. I hope she turns up."

Audrey took out a business card. "I'd be grateful if you could ask any of Sally's friends to call me. You never know what might help."

"Sure." Ash took her card and hurried off.

Donna sighed. "That was a bust."

"Yes and no. Interesting question about her date being someone from here. You thinking they met online and found out they go to the same gym and got to know each other here?"

"Or he could have met her here and then found her online, but the first option is more likely. He could be here right now, watching us."

The thought chilled Audrey. "That's a cheery thought. Come on. Let's go."

It was good to be outside in the fresh air. Audrey looked around to make sure no one was listening. "What Ash said is all in keeping with what we know. Sally was a regular. Her life was scheduled and ran like clockwork. That makes it easy for someone to know your routine. When you go out. When you're alone. Except Sally went missing after a date that no one knew about, not after the gym or her morning walk or any of her other regular activities."

Donna looked stumped as well.

Audrey opened the car. "Why does a woman who tells the people closest to her every movement go out with a man no one knows and not tell a soul?"

Donna answered, "Maybe she didn't think they'd approve. Or if he's married, they need to keep it a secret. Sixty percent of married men report having an affair sometime in their marriage. Except he wouldn't be online and risk someone seeing him."

They walked in silence until Donna finally said, "Maybe she got sick of bringing home guys that didn't work out, and she wanted to make sure he was the one. I get that. Dating can be exhausting."

Was it as simple as that? Did Sally want to make sure he was right before bringing him into her world? Olive might be easy, but Bill could be intimidating. Audrey opened the car, and they climbed in. "I get not telling her parents or the boys, but her best friend?"

"Yeah, that's weird. I always tell someone."

Audrey was pleased to hear that.

Donna sat up, excited. "What if he asked Sally to keep their relationship a secret? He could have made up some story about why, and when she agreed, he knew there would be no trace back to him? If she really liked him, she might do what he asked. It would explain why he hasn't come forward."

Love or the prospect of love could do strange things to people, but would Sally agree not to tell anyone about her date because he asked? It wasn't something they could solve right now.

9

She must have dozed off but was still stuck in a barrel. Was she suffocating? She breathed in the stale air, filling her lungs, and the panic subsided. Water. Her mouth and throat were dry. A dull, throbbing sensation had begun on one side of her head and radiated around to the other side.

She had watched a documentary about a hiker who went without water for days. No water could also lead to more serious symptoms such as rapid heartbeat, confusion, and even seizures. She couldn't think like that. *Focus.* She had to get out.

Frustrated, she kicked and slammed her hands against the top and sides of the barrel. "Help. Help. Let me out!' Nothing. Her back and legs throbbed. Shifting from side to side helped, but if she stopped moving, it returned. What day was it? She was losing track of time. Sunday, perhaps? Oh god, her parents. When she hadn't turned up yesterday, they would know something was wrong, but by now they must be frantic. They would have everyone out looking for her. The idea stopped the rising panic.

But what if her mum had a bad night and went wandering again? What if her father forgot about coffee and to ring Rick? Her mother's illness was taking its toll on her father, who looked more tired and drawn each day. Her aunt had agreed to take her brother, Sally's father, away for a week. Sally would move in to care for her mother. Her father just had to agree. He might forget about coffee for one day, but not two, surely?

Her friend Di. They hadn't spoken this week, and now she was in Queensland. Once upon a time, they knew each other's every movement, talking every night after school.

Those days were gone. Di had tried to fix her up with a friend of her husband's, Charlie, and when that didn't work out she suggested Sally might be looking for Mr Perfect, who didn't exist. Di might be right, but she didn't want to settle. She would rather be on her own.

But it meant she had stopped telling Di about her dates until things were further along. But if her date had anything to do with this, no one knew who he was or how to locate him. Right now, this felt like a huge mistake.

A thought chilled her. Had anyone even known she was going on a date? She had told Lucas and Trish, but they wouldn't know she was missing until Monday. Her mother? Had she told her? She couldn't remember. Her brother Rick. Yes, she'd told Rick. Relief washed over her.

She'd spoken to him on Friday when he called into work to collect the free samples she'd organised. Thank God for her brother and his love of a freebie. He'd asked why she looked so happy, and that was when she told him about her date. Relief flooded over her.

She'd kept her voice down. Gavin was nearby, and she knew how he felt about her. It was one thing to decline his advances, another to rub it in his face. It would be so easy if she felt that way about Gavin, but she didn't. There was no physical attraction or chemistry. No romantic feelings or desire for intimacy. Her parents liked him, or her mother at least.

The day he took her hand and didn't let go meant she had to tell him. Above all else, they were friends, and that would never change. The words mumbled out like a babbling brook while he stood slumped with a broken heart, his shoulders heavy with disappointment.

Only when he walked away did she see his clenched fists and realise how angry he was. Now that she thought about it, they hadn't spoken much since then.

Rick had told her to be careful with her date. Sally was normally the one telling him that, but it was nice he cared. She made him promise not to say anything, but once they realised she was missing, he would tell Craig, and they would start looking for her. Craig, the connector with his mean wife and addiction to social media, would put the word out. Perhaps even organise a search.

Her spirits lifted. She pictured them looking for her. The first place they would look was her home. No clues there. Then work and the gym, and it was anyone's guess after that. She imagined them coming for her. Their voices as they tried to find her. Faint at first, their voices would grow louder and more frantic when they spotted the barrel.

Get her out.

They would need a tool to lift the lid off the barrel. A hammer and chisel to remove the ring and to tap the staves to loosen the lid. Someone would carefully lift her out, and she could spread her limbs out. Oh, how she wanted to be upright. Water. Someone would hand her a glass of cold water.

The glass would be cold and smooth, her hands shaking as she lifted it to her lips. It would taste of nothing. Not sweet nor bitter, just plain, beautiful water. As she sipped, it would hit the back of her throat then eventually her stomach.

What would that feel like? She'd never really thought about it until now. Warm and soothing? It would be the best drink she'd ever had.

Eventually, she would be driven home and get to stand under her shower and let the warm water fall over her until it ran cold. They would all stay up talking until there were no more words. Eventually she would fall into her crisp sheets and sleep.

It wouldn't be long now. Her family and friends would find her. And when she found out who put her in a barrel, boy would she have something to say. In the meantime, she had to keep moving. Starting with her head, she adjusted it slowly forward, careful not to make any sudden movements, then to the side, the back, and the other side.

Next was her right arm. Slowly, she moved it up, down, forward, and back. They were on the way. She had to wait.

10

M onday

"It just keeps coming."

Audrey looked over at an exasperated Donna, who was reading the comments on the newspaper's social media page. Sally Child's disappearance had struck a chord with local women, seemingly falling into two camps. Some wondered if the Peninsula had a maniac on the loose, while others suggested she was with her date and urged people to give the poor woman her privacy.

Audrey did a final read-over of her piece on Sally Child.

Each morning Sally Child visits her parents and brings them coffee. When she didn't arrive on Saturday morning, they quickly knew something was wrong.

The people who thought Sally was with her date were about to be silenced.

Donna spun her chair towards Audrey. "Want to see what I found on her work bestie, Gavin?"

Their fellow journalist, Stan, who had one eye on retirement, looked up. "Don't tell me. You know his tax file number and what he has for breakfast."

Stan loved poking fun at Donna, but it worked both ways.

Donna mock glared at him. "Not quite, old man, but there are things here to work with."

Audrey walked over to her computer. On the screen was a photo of Sally and Gavin at the brewery. Gavin was an inch or two taller than Sally, so five-seven or eight. Short for a man. Plenty of women dated shorter men. He had brown hair, a stocky build, but wasn't fat. Ordinary. Average came to mind. Harmless? They were holding up a single beer bottle each like proud new parents.

"Hashtag new release," said Donna. "There are a few photos like that. These guys have lots of new releases. But then I found this one at the dumpling place on the highway."

"Best dumplings on the Peninsula," said Stan, who prided himself on knowing the best local eating experiences. Audrey liked that his recommendations could come from canteens, service stations, or restaurants with stars. It was all about the quality, not the venue.

Gavin and Sally were sitting in front of a plate of Chinese dumplings in Bennington. "Someone took the photo for them. A special occasion, maybe?"

Sally had both hands on the table, facing forward. Gavin's hands were also on the table, but his left hand was turned towards her.

"But look at his face. He's smiling, but his eyes are in a world of pain."

All Audrey could see was someone who looked exhausted. "He could be tired."

Donna frowned. "But it means something to him because he posted it."

"Agree."

Environment was a critical factor in eliciting information. Interrogation rooms were intentionally austere to make people want to get out of there. But places with warm memories could also be effective. She could ask Gavin if he wanted to have some dumplings. "Any other photos?"

Donna scrolled through Gavin's other posts, which all appeared to be taken at work. "Not much going on outside of work except for this one with Sally's folks."

Gavin was standing in the middle of Bill and Olive. It looked like any other happy family shot, except they weren't his family. What did Olive and Bill have to say about him?

The door opened and footsteps climbed the stairs. It was their Editor Eve with her poodle, Phillip. "Morning all."

Mornings all round. They were all fond of the dog, but mainly because Eve was more relaxed in his presence. Donna gave Phillip a warm pat, then sanitised her hands while Eve fixed her normally pristine grey bob from the effects of the wind outside.

Looking at Audrey, she asked, "What's the latest on Sally Child?"

Eve liked to stay across stories that were delicate and complex. By delicate, she meant they involved either a missing or dead person. By complex, she was referring to the police and other bodies of authority being involved. Prior to joining the *Gazette*, Eve had worked for one of the dailies when both Jill Meagher and Eurydice Dixon were found murdered. Her interest ran deeper this time, judging by the call Audrey had received last night requesting an update.

"Do the police have any idea who her date is yet?"

"Not yet. Sally had an eHarmony profile, so the police might look there."

Eve sighed. "That could take a while. We need to keep information online and on socials up to date and hope somebody comes forward with something. Set up a page, 'Help us find Sally Child.' Cover all the platforms. Somebody knows something."

"Sally has a close friend at work called Gavin. I was going to call in to the brewery this afternoon and see if I can catch him."

"I take it the police have spoken to him?" Eve's insistence on protocol annoyed her at times, but she had no choice but to go along with it.

Audrey had spoken to Cath Maguire last night, asking if they had spoken to him. "Yes, they have."

Eve nodded. If the police had spoken to Gavin, Audrey was fine to proceed.

Donna chimed in. "Sally's bosses think he wanted to be more than friends."

44

Eve had also cautioned Donna about jumping onto a theory too early. "And you think he might have been jealous and had something to do with her disappearance?"

Eve's expression was deadpan, but Audrey detected an edge to her question. "I'd prefer we answer that after I've spoken with him. I'd also like to see her parents to determine what they have to say about him."

Eve frowned. Interviewing the parents so early in an investigation was venturing into precarious territory.

"We got on well yesterday, and I will only ask about Sally's friend."

This seemed to work; Eve picked up Philip's lead. "This must be awful for them. Let's hope this has a better ending. Anything else?"

Audrey shook her head. "I'll send you the latest piece on Sally now."

"I'll get on to it straight away."

And with that, Eve headed into her office and settled Phillip into his bed then closed the door.

Donna looked up at her. "Please take me with you."

Suddenly, Eve's door opened. "Oh, and I'd like to run a piece on safety for women. Top ten tips or something like that." Eve looked at Donna. "Maybe you could take that one."

Donna lit up. Audrey had suggested it was time to give Donna her own stories to complete, but it hadn't eventuated until now. "On it."

Eve closed the door.

Donna clapped her hands, excited. "I can't believe she gave me my own piece."

Stan glanced at Audrey. "Oh. Junior's taking off the training wheels. Better make sure you do a good job."

A flash of worry crossed Donna's face before she turned back to her computer. "You better believe it."

Audrey smiled at Stan. They both knew she would. She was also grateful since she wanted to fly solo today. Olive and Bill were more likely to speak to one person, and it would make it easier to build rapport with Gavin. "Next time."

11

Sally's parents lived at the Eliza James facility. With its smart reception desk, modern light grey carpet and furnishings, it reminded Audrey more of a resort than an aged care facility. The only clue it was the latter was an elderly man being supported by a nurse farther along the corridor. Competition for residents was fierce these days, so operators had to lift their game both in terms of the environment and level of care.

Audrey approached the reception desk. A woman in her fifties looked up from her computer and smiled. "Can I help you?"

"Yes. My name is Audrey Lord. I'd like to see Mr and Mrs Child. I met them yesterday." She left out the part about being a journalist. People's responses could go either way.

The woman dialled a number. "Good morning. There's an Audrey Lord to see you." The woman listened. "She said she met you yesterday."

Audrey had called ahead, but she was relieved to hear her say, "Very well. I'll send her around."

The woman hung up and laid a map of the facility on the desk. "This is us here. If you go back out the front doors and turn left and then take the first left, it's on the right-hand side. Number fourteen."

Audrey took the map. "Thanks."

Following the instructions, she passed a strip of smart, single-level units. An elderly woman who reminded her of Betty White with her cheery face weeding the tiny garden at the front of her property looked over. "Morning. Beautiful day, isn't it?"

"It is a beautiful day."

Except that the couple she was about to meet had a missing daughter.

Number fourteen looked like all the other units with its brick and light grey rendered walls and single-car garage. A small path led to the front door.

Bill Child was waiting with the security door open. "See you found the place."

Audrey held up the map. "Thanks for seeing me. This is a lovely facility."

Bill's lips pursed. "We used to be on three-quarters of an acre with a beautiful garden, but I couldn't manage on my own. I can't stop Olive from getting out, but knowing she can't get far provides us both great comfort. I can't fault the level of care. Worth every penny."

Audrey followed Bill into the living room. At the far end was a small but tidy kitchen.

Bill walked behind the counter. "Tea or coffee? It's a fresh pot."

Audrey spotted the pot of drip filter coffee. "Coffee. Black, thanks."

Olive walked into the kitchen. "Hello, dear. My name is Olive."

Olive didn't recognise her.

"Hello. Audrey Lord." Audrey shook Olive's soft hand.

Bill's face was stony. "Take a seat on the sofa. I'll bring the drinks over."

Olive sat on a comfortable-looking brown leather sofa and gestured for Audrey to sit next to her. "Bill tells me you're here to help us find Sally."

The optimism in the way she said it was heartbreaking. "I'm here to see if I can help, yes."

Bill put the drinks on a small coffee table and sat opposite. "So what would you like to know?"

She imagined some people found Bill's manner brisk, but she

would dispense with niceties as well if either of her children were missing.

"I understand Sally's best friend at work was Gavin?"

Olive sat up on high alert, looking at her husband. "They've been close friends since she took the job. We like Gavin, don't we Bill?"

Bill was more circumspect. "He seems a nice enough fellow. Sally brought him here a few times, and he helped with a couple of maintenance things around the place. I can't get up a ladder like I used to."

Olive nestled closer to Audrey, like they were two girlfriends about to share a secret. "We thought they might be dating, but Sally said they were just friends. I couldn't see the problem. They got on well, worked in the same industry, like Bill and I did. My work was in imaging physics, where we studied the physical world from the atomic scale through to imaging the human body." There was a sharp mind in there, making her situation even more tragic. "Sometimes I think young people are too fussy these days, looking for Mr or Mrs Perfect."

"Do you think Gavin felt that way towards Sally?"

"Yes. I could tell he did," said Olive. "But Bill wasn't convinced. Were you, Bill?"

Bill sat back, considering his response. "I don't enjoy extrapolating without facts. In my experience, if a man wants to date someone, he will ask her out to a restaurant or make it clear he wants something more. As far as I'm aware, Gavin did nothing to indicate he wanted to be more than friends."

Was Bill correct, or had he missed the signs? Or had Sally not told them?

"Has Gavin been to see you or been in touch since Sally went missing?"

Bill gave Audrey a tiny shake of the head, but he didn't seem to think there was anything unusual in that.

Audrey looked at Olive, but her focus was on something out the window.

Bill sat forward. "He's been a good friend to Sally. Helping her around the house and being her plus one to a couple of weddings, but they're just friends, despite Olive wishing it was more."

Something about Gavin's behaviour niggled.

"Where does Gavin live?" Audrey knew, but it was worth checking in case any new information became available.

"In the Boroughs. He rents a place there. He offered Sally a room before she bought her place, but the following week, her place came up for sale with a short settlement, so it didn't seem worth it. She thought sharing a house might risk their friendship, so it gave her an excuse not to take up his offer without hurting his feelings. Why do you want to know that?"

She had to tread carefully. "I was curious. Sometimes I wonder how people afford a house, even renting, on one income these days."

It was a bad sidestep but appeared to work.

Audrey had a picture of Sally from her family and friends, but to really know someone, you had to see their home. "This might seem like an odd request, but I wondered whether we could visit Sally's home. With you, of course. I wouldn't touch anything, but I find a person's home gives me a real sense of who they are."

Bill sipped his coffee, considering the idea. "Have you ever lost a child?"

"Temporarily, yes." Audrey's heart thudded at the memory of Josh going missing at Chadstone Shopping Centre. The ten minutes until a store assistant found him hiding under a rack of men's pants was one of the worst experiences of her life.

"Then you remember how scary the feeling is. Every minute since she's been gone feels like that, so if you feel that visiting her home will help, we can go."

Bill stood. "Olive."

Olive snapped out of wherever she was and turned to face them.

"We're going to Sally's."

Olive brightened. "I knew she'd come back. I'll grab my handbag."

As Olive hurried off, Bill watched his wife sadly.

12

Sally Child lived in a blonde-brick veneer house on a quarter-acre block in Bennington South. The front garden consisted of a recently trimmed lawn and a garden bed under the main window.

Bill was in the passenger seat. "You can park in the driveway."

Audrey pulled into the concrete driveway. Bill climbed out and opened the back door to help Olive. "Don't leave your valuables in the car."

"But we're not doing any shopping," said Olive, confused.

Bill didn't bother repeating the instruction, but Olive got the message, picked up her bag, and climbed out.

"Wait here."

The constant issuing of instructions reminded Audrey of when the kids were little. How exhausting having to go through that again at Bill's age. He walked to the side of the house and knelt down to what looked like a key safe.

Audrey locked the car and came and stood alongside Olive, who mumbled, "Zero, nine, one, two. Zero. Nine. One, two. Zero. Nine. One. Two." The key safe code?

He closed the key safe. "We used to have a key, but…"

"I kept losing it." Olive looked down like a scolded child.

"It wasn't just you, love. Rick's girlfriend broke into Sally's home.

After that, Sally didn't want any stray keys floating around, so we came up with this solution."

"Where is Rick's girlfriend now?"

Bill stepped onto the porch. "She lives in the UK now."

"Good riddance," mumbled Olive.

Audrey stifled a grin. No love lost there.

Bill opened the front door. "We put deadlocks on all the doors and windows. Can't be too safe these days."

Audrey followed Bill and Olive into the front hall. The place was pristine, with spotless white walls and timber floorboards in excellent condition. The faint scent of vanilla enhanced the fresh feel of the place. On the right was a master bedroom and to the left was the living and dining room. The furnishings were generic. The IKEA catalogue sitting on the bench at home came to mind.

On a dresser were framed photos. One was of Sally with a woman her age. As Audrey leaned in to take a closer look, Olive stood along-side her. "That's her best friend, Di. They've been friends since primary school."

Di had shoulder-length brown hair, clear skin, and wore black exercise pants and a spotless zipped-up mint-green jacket. She was due back today, so Audrey was hoping to speak with her soon.

Another photo showed Sally at work with colleagues, judging by the barrels in the background. Lucas was on the far left, then Sally, Trish, and other work colleagues. A stone-faced Gavin was on the other side of the group. They were each holding a bottle of beer. A new release, perhaps?

The third picture was of the four members of her family. Olive repositioned the photo so it lined up with the others. "The police were here yesterday."

Bill was looking at her. "Where would you like to start?"

Kitchens and living rooms were the heart of people's homes but often set up for friends and family. In contrast, the bedroom and bath-room were private spaces where you got to know someone. "Sally's bedroom, if that's okay."

Bill pointed to the master bedroom. "In there."

"Look, Bill. It's the postman." Olive pointed out the front window. "I'll go get the mail."

"I'll grab it." Bill looked at Audrey. "Please don't touch anything."

"No. Of course not."

Audrey entered Sally's room. Olive followed and sat on the bed. The queen-size bed had a white duvet, charcoal throw rug, and white stacked pillows flanked by two timber bedside tables.

Sally slept on the side closest to the wardrobe, going by the Nora Roberts book on the bedside table. Opposite the bed was a timber chest of drawers. There were no photos or other personal items on display, which seemed odd.

"She's done a lovely job on the place. Sally's always been good with money, even when she was a little girl." Olive rubbed her hand across the duvet and lowered her voice. "Don't tell anyone, but she got most things here on special. She's got a real eye for a bargain."

Audrey smiled, warming even more to the woman. "It's a good skill to have. Do you mind if I have a look in her wardrobe?"

Olive shrugged. "I suppose so."

Audrey opened the closet. Jackets, shirts, and dresses hung neatly on the same-style timber hangers. At the bottom was a selection of shoes: two pairs of ASICS runners, dress shoes, casual shoes. Nothing too high-end, consistent with a woman in her thirties with expenses other than clothes. On the top shelf were hoodies and jumpers folded into neat piles.

Olive stood next to Audrey, taking her hand. The gesture took her by surprise. She could feel the tsunami of emotions in the woman's grip, from gratitude to pure fear, and right now, more than anything, she wanted to help find Sally for Olive and Bill. Audrey waited for Olive to release her grip.

There was no ensuite in the main bedroom, but she was keen to see the bathroom, the room where a person got ready before meeting the rest of the world. "Can we look at the bathroom?"

"Yes. It's a lovely room."

Olive led them into the next room along the hallway. Running the width of the wall, the bath looked original. Audrey liked the idea of a bath but always felt like she needed a shower afterwards, which seemed to defeat the purpose. The shower had new tiles and a glass screen. Judging by the products on a shelf, Sally was also more of a shower person. Audrey was keen to have a rummage around before Bill got back and without Olive watching.

"Could I trouble you for a glass of water, please?"

"Of course. I'll be right back." Olive left to get her drink.

Moving fast, Audrey opened the bathroom cabinets. There was the usual assortment of hair products, deodorants, perfume. A small cup held packets of medication. Voltaren. Panadol. Nurofen. No prescriptions. The plumbing clunked as a tap ran in the kitchen. She opened the drawers in the vanity. Inside was a hairdryer, hair straightener, and liquid soap refills for the shower. All consistent with Sally being a good shopper who bought items on sale. In the corner was a cobalt-blue toilet bag. Inside were a spare toothbrush, a comb, and a nail file. She checked the side pockets. The first was empty. Bill wiped his feet on the front door mat and stepped inside.

"Sorry. Got stuck talking to her neighbour who wanted to know if there'd been any developments."

Audrey put the toilet bag back, closed the drawer, and stepped into the hallway to greet Bill. "Sally's done a lovely job decorating the place."

Bill looked around for Olive.

"Olive is getting me a glass of water."

A flash of concern crossed Bill's face, but then it was gone.

"I might look at the kitchen, if that's okay?"

Bill nodded and walked ahead.

Olive was at the kitchen tap, staring at the garden as the glass of water in her hand overflowed. Bill gently took the glass and turned off the tap. Tipping some of the water out, he wiped the sides and bottom with a tea towel and handed it to Audrey without meeting her eye. The insidious disease was exhausting enough for the carers without having to deal with the reactions of others.

"Thanks." Audrey took the water and sipped.

On the bench were a small fruit bowl with green apples and an orange. Audrey had read a study that showed people with a fruit bowl on the bench tended to weigh less. She didn't know if it was true, but it fit someone like Sally, who was fit and healthy.

Audrey spotted the fridge. You could tell a lot about a person by what was inside. "Do you mind if I take a look in the fridge?"

"I don't see why not," said Bill.

Audrey opened the door. On the top shelf were butter and a packet of grated cheese. Some ready-made meals on the second shelf. A small selection of fruit and vegetables in the crisper. For a single woman, it was well-stocked.

Bill read her thoughts. "Sally didn't like things going to waste."

Audrey closed the door.

"Look at all the lemons, Bill," said Olive. "We should take some with us."

In the backyard was a lemon tree bursting with fruit. Audrey's attention was more focused on a metal garden shed in the corner of the yard. It was secured with a padlock. "Does Sally keep much in the shed?"

Bill shook his head. "Only the mower and a few tools. There are some tubs with old books and things like that. We had a look inside, and it's all still there. She doesn't enjoy going in. Thinks it's full of spiders, even though the Huntsman are more scared of her."

Audrey wasn't so sure. She wasn't a fan and once heard them described as like a man's hairy hand running on the roof. They might be scared, but that didn't stop them running towards humans.

"She never did like Huntsman spiders, did she, Bill?"

Olive was already speaking in the past tense.

"No, love. She doesn't," said Bill, keen to stay in the present.

Audrey was keen to look inside, but Bill looked exhausted, and she had to get to the brewery to catch Gavin.

"Was there anything else you wanted to look at?"

Audrey took a final look around. Sally took pride in her home. There was fresh food in her fridge and none of the usual signs that she had planned to go away. If anything, the visit made the situation feel even more grim. She sensed Bill and Olive waiting for her.

"I don't think so, but thanks for letting me have a look around."

"I hope this helps," said Bill, gently taking Olive's arm and leading her towards the front door. The way Bill cared for Olive was sweet. On the way out, Audrey tapped Zero, nine, one, two into her phone.

13

Audrey walked into the brewery. The place was empty, with tables and chairs moved to the side, giving it an eerie, cavernous feeling. It was a stark contrast to the weekend.

"Hello?" She felt like an intruder.

There was no response. Where was everyone?

At the end of the bar was a door. An office, perhaps? She approached, but as she got closer she could make out voices arguing. "I'm so sick of this!" It was Trish.

"You're sick of it?" Was that Lucas? "Things are getting back on track, and now this happens. What about the kids? If anyone finds out…"

It was Trish again. "We'll cross that bridge if we need to. You've got to keep it together for all our sakes. Can you do that?"

Silence.

"Come here," said Trish.

Were they talking about the business or Sally?

A truck with Bennington Brewery on the side turned into the laneway. Was Gavin driving? She hurried outside, but it was someone else.

The driver leaned over and wound down the window. "We're not open on Mondays, love."

"I was looking for Gavin. Is he around?"

Curious, the man tilted his head to one side. "He was ahead of me, so if he's not here, he's gone. You'll find him down at the pub. Goes there for a quick coldie after work."

Bennington Pub was full of tradies and drivers who congregated each afternoon for the day's debrief. People went for the social side of things as much as the beer, which he could probably have at work, albeit on his own. Maybe Gavin wasn't such an introvert after all? But if he'd just left, Audrey had to move fast. "Thanks."

Bennington Bar was busy, mostly populated by men in high-vis vests over shorts or overalls. The older ones sat at the bar while the younger ones stood at high tables sipping their beer and checking the time. The ones with kids would need to leave soon to help with bathing or to fire up the barbecue.

Audrey scanned the bar for Gavin. A few people looked over but returned to their beer and conversations.

She approached the bar. "Hi. I'm looking for Gavin Cox. He's a regular here."

The man in his early thirties, a less handsome version of Dave Grohl, front man for the Foo Fighters, scanned the bar. "Yeah. He was here before." And then yelled, "Anyone seen Gav?"

A man in a high-vis vest with ruddy red cheeks stepped forward. "He just left. Probably gone to get dumplings. Eats the damn things like Maltesers."

There was only one place in Bennington that sold dumplings, and it was located opposite the hotel on the other side of the road.

The barman smiled. "Everyone knows everything about everyone around here."

"Thanks." Audrey hurried out.

The Tasty Dumpling Restaurant was halfway along a small shopping strip on the highway. Chinese writing and red windows made it easy to spot. A bell tinkled as she opened the door. Inside were half a dozen tables and seating at the rear for takeaway customers. Gavin was sitting on a bench at the rear, waiting for takeaway. He was tapping into his phone, but his face was expressionless. A small Asian woman placed a plastic bag with half a dozen containers on the counter. That was a lot of dumplings for one person.

A strange thought occurred to her. What if Sally was hiding out at Gavin's? Was she fearful of her date and wanting to lie low for a few days? It would explain why Gavin wasn't at the search. But Sally wouldn't do that to her parents. She dismissed the idea and approached him. "Hi, Gavin?"

He looked up, surprised. "Yeah."

"My name is Audrey Lord. I'm a journalist with the Gazette."

Gavin hurried past her. "I'm not talking to any journalist," and then he was out the door. Not this again.

Audrey hurried after him. "I want to ask you a few questions about Sally. I believe you and she are good friends."

He didn't respond and kept walking.

"I've been working with Craig and the family. I'm trying to help. Olive and Bill took me to Sally's today."

Gavin hurried across the highway and ran towards the pub's carpark with impressive speed. What the hell was this guy's problem? Did he hate journalists or have something to hide? Or both?

Audrey waited for traffic to pass, but by the time she made it across he had disappeared into the carpark. There was only one way out of the hotel complex, and that meant passing Audrey's car in the middle island. She quickly climbed in and waited. She didn't know what he drove, but he shouldn't be difficult to spot. Moments later, a white Ford Falcon sedan sped out of the carpark with Gavin at the wheel. He didn't see her, so she let him pass and then pulled out to follow.

Ten minutes later, Gavin predictably turned into the Boroughs. Bennington was divided into money on the hill, those in the middle, and the Boroughs. The place permanently looked like it needed a good hose-down and scrub.

Good people lived here, but also plenty of bad ones. Like Audrey's nemesis, Sharon Miller, the woman who'd run her out of town decades earlier. Despite Audrey never having lived here, the area always evoked lots of emotions, and only a few good ones.

Moments later, Gavin pulled into the driveway of a small blonde-brick home with a balding lawn and an overgrown yucca plant. A single garage was separate from the house and at the rear of the property. Audrey parked in front of the house next door. Gavin walked inside with his bag of dumplings. Audrey considered her options. She could knock on the door, but she didn't picture that going any differently to their earlier encounter.

If he recognised her from the dumpling shop and realised she had followed him, he might lodge a complaint with the police. Cath Maguire would call, and if she was annoyed enough, she'd get Eve involved. Mark was home, and she had no desire to upset their anniversary.

But what if Sally was in there? There was no harm in telling Cath Maguire she had spotted Gavin buying enough food for more than one person. She dialled her number.

Cath answered. "Hi there."

Her tone was friendly but clipped. She was busy.

"Sally's best friend, Gavin?"

Cath responded, "Shy guy who lives on his own in the Boroughs and holds a torch for Sally. What about him?"

Audrey smiled. "I tried to speak with him, but he avoided me like the plague."

Cath laughed. "Sorry. You must be used to that, though."

People run away from journalists for a myriad of reasons; fear of being misquoted, negative consequences from an employer, general lack of trust, or simply a desire for privacy.

"Yes, but I'm trying to help find his best friend. You'd think he'd be more helpful. But I'm ringing because I saw him coming out of the dumpling place on the highway with enough for more than one person."

Cath would annoyingly suggest he might be hungry or bought enough for a few meals like lots of people did.

"And so you think he has Sally Child holed up in his place like Kathy Bates in *Misery* and is feeding her dumplings?"

No. Maybe. The guy was odd, so anything was possible. Even so, it was important that Cath didn't think she was jumping to conclusions.

"I wanted to ask whether anyone has been out to his place."

Cath sounded wary. "I sent a couple of the team out earlier, but hang on…"

Cath had once lamented the poor quality of the junior recruits coming through the force. Audrey promised to never repeat that, but she had also never forgotten it.

Cath came back on the line. "They said the place is a tip, but they didn't find anything."

Audrey looked at the garage. "Did they check the garage out back?"

Judging by the silence, that was a no.

14

Audrey walked in to find Mark at the table, showing the kids photos on his iPad.

"That looks mean." Josh was incredulous. He often was at his father's exciting life, as he saw it, out on the rigs. It hadn't always been that way. At first, he had nightmares that his dad would be swept away into the ocean. Mark had done a good job explaining safety protocols, which put him at ease.

Mark laughed heartily, his deep chuckle filling the room. "It was ferocious."

He always looked happy and upbeat the first night. It was the high of finally stopping work. The crash would come tomorrow.

Audrey put her bag on the bench. "Hello, you."

Every time Mark came home, it felt like they were starting over, because in some small way they were. Audrey had to get used to another adult in the house and in her bed. Mark had to get used to living with three people and not hundreds. The kids to having their father back. It was an adjustment for all of them.

Mark pushed his chair back. "Here she is."

Freshly showered, he was wearing the pale blue and white shirt she bought him, with jeans. Wrapping his arms around her, he smelt of the vanilla bath but then, as he held her tighter, his own unique musky smell. The one that was comforting and evoked years of memories and shared experiences.

He kissed her on the lips. He tasted warm and sweet, like honey, with a hint of spice and a tiny splash of toothpaste. Was that a new mouthwash? Neither was one for long, passionate kisses in front of the kids. Audrey was always the one to pull away first. There would be time for more of that later.

"Enough of that," said Josh, grinning.

Mark gave her a knowing look. Josh had stopped saying how gross it was to see his parents kiss. Did it mean there was a girl somewhere?

Beth's expression was harder to read. With her lips slightly pursed and her chin up, she looked like someone who had spotted an unusual bug on the window.

Mark walked back to the table. "I'm showing the kids photos of the storm coming in when we left."

Audrey leaned in and peered at the vicious-looking sky, the enormous blue-green waves, and bobbing in amongst all that, the rig, at the mercy of the elements. Somewhere inside were the poor workers trying not to be sick, and with the satellite dish unable to keep a fix due to the bouncing around, waiting it out with no TV. It was her idea of hell.

She gulped. "Lucky you got out when you did."

Mark looked at the photo and frowned. "Tell me about it."

He put the iPad away.

"Suppose I better have a shower," said Audrey.

Mark looked up at her, eyes bright. "Where are we going?" Then at his outfit. "Is this okay?"

One question at a time. "It's a surprise, and yes."

"What are we having for dinner?" Josh asked. "Can we come?"

Mark put both hands on Josh's shoulders. Josh smiled up at his father. "Not tonight. But I was thinking we could do a few things together this week. See a movie. Maybe a bit of shopping on the weekend."

Where was this coming from?

Josh grinned. "Sounds great. Hey, Dad, there's this new Korean chicken place we should try."

Audrey felt guilty. Both kids had been asking her to try Bennington's newest eating place.

"We've been asking Mum to take us there for weeks," Beth said with an eye roll.

Audrey flinched. Mum had to work, drive both kids around, and run a house full-time with only occasional help. Oh, and then work on the weekend to help find a woman who was missing. There wasn't a lot of time left to be the fun parent.

"Your mother has enough to do, but let's see if we can all go."

Audrey looked at Mark, grateful. "I really need to have a shower and," turning to Josh, "in answer to your question, there's a packet of pasta in the fridge and sauce in the cupboard."

"Cheese?" Josh put grated cheese on everything he could.

"There's plenty of cheese."

Audrey walked into the bedroom. Mark's suitcase had exploded on the bed, and a small pile of dirty washing was on the floor. She was never going to be the kind of wife who could look at that and feel only joy that her husband was home, but there was no irritation either. She smiled. Progress.

Audrey stood under the shower, letting the hot water cascade over her, eyes closed. The water tried to wash away the day until: Where are you, Sally Child? Kidnapped and alive? Or dead and lying somewhere? Or worse, never to be found. People went missing all the time. Some turned up, while others' faces became permanent fixtures on missing persons posters. Not knowing was the worst.

Audrey had seen what it did to people. Destroyed lives. Endless years spent searching. Olive wouldn't remember soon, but Bill would be haunted by Sally's disappearance until the day he died. Were they missing something? She was interested to see how things were at the brewery tonight.

"It's good to be back."

Mark's voice jolted her. She wiped a small section of glass to see him unpacking his toilet bag. "It's good to have you back."

It was a perfunctory response but all she could come up with now. They hadn't talked much this trip due to a combination of Mark's shifts and parent-teacher interviews, so they had plenty of catching up to do. She listened to the clinking of items being put back into drawers and vanity and turned off the water. Mark handed her a towel as she stepped onto the bathmat. "Thanks."

Audrey dried herself while Mark filled her in on the lives of a couple of the guys she had never met but knew the names of and what was new on the menu. Food was a big deal on the rig, and the honey garlic pork chops had been this trip's favourite. Audrey had given up trying to compete with the chefs and restaurant-quality meals on offer.

By the time she was dry, Mark had begun putting his clothes away. It wasn't something he did the first day back, but she wasn't going to complain. He seemed brighter. Was something going on?

Mark didn't look at her as he put away his socks. "Beth said you've been out all weekend."

Was Beth keeping tabs on her movements? That would be a first.

"I had that reunion I told you about Friday, and the rest of the weekend was taken up helping look for a woman who's missing."

Audrey gave him the headlines as she slipped on a dress. Sally Child. Mornington. Out of character.

Mark kissed her on the lips. "I hope she turns up."

Was that all he had to say? Mark didn't know Sally or her friends or family. She was another stranger who had gone missing. So why was she disappointed with his response?

"Me too."

She could manage the zip with some effort, but it was easier to get him to help, so she turned to face him. He kissed her back before pulling the zipper up. "Looking forward to getting that off you later."

She smiled but wasn't done on Sally yet. "I've met her family. They're really lovely people."

Mark stepped back. "Let's not talk about work tonight."

Audrey bristled. She tended to become consumed with work, but feeling petulant, she thought if he showed a little more interest, she wouldn't need to. Needing a moment alone, she walked into the ensuite, hoping he wouldn't follow her.

"Sure."

A set of keys clinked, and the bedroom door closed. Taking out her makeup, she applied a thin shield of foundation. There it was again. The palpable sense of disappointment. But not at Mark or the kids or anyone else. It was at the person staring back at her in the mirror.

Audrey Lord. Part-time investigative journalist. Despite helping to solve two of the Peninsula's biggest crimes, that was all she would ever be. To her family, the public, and to herself. How long was she going to settle for that?

15

The brewery was back to being busy when Audrey and Mark arrived. The inside tables were full, and people were seated at most communal tables outside.

Mark's face lit up, and the corners of his mouth stretched into a broad smile. "This place is great."

Pleased he liked it, she spotted an unoccupied end near a group of middle-aged men who didn't look too rowdy and turned to Mark. "Grab that end over there, and I'll surprise you."

Audrey approached the bar. Jake handed a customer a paddle with a selection of beers in it, took his money, and turned to Audrey.

She wondered if he'd recognise her. "Hi. We met the other day."

He did. "Hey. The bosses aren't here, though."

Audrey felt a pang of disappointment. She was hoping to get a read on Trish and Lucas after hearing them argue earlier. "Is it normally this busy on a Monday?"

"First Monday of the month, we showcase our new ranges."

All the more reason for Trish and Lucas to be here? "I thought they would want to be here for that?"

"They normally would be, but one of the kids has a concert on."

Jake's tone hinted that he didn't think that was sufficient reason.

"I'm actually here with my husband. Can I have a tasting paddle and an IPA?" Audrey normally drank sparkling or red wine but occasionally liked a beer, and Mark would find it more fun if she joined him. "How are things going without Sally?"

"Lucas has been doing Sal's job, so it's a bit crazy," said Jake. "We're all hoping she turns up, you know."

Jake put the drinks down and pushed the terminal towards Audrey. There was good money in beer. He headed off to serve another group of customers.

Audrey placed the paddle down in front of Mark and took a seat. "Try the IPA, which is what I have, and we can compare notes."

Mark selected the IPA, and they clinked glasses. This was nice.

"We've got something else to celebrate," said Mark, taking a sip and then carefully placing his beer down.

Oh. There was something going on. "What's that?"

Mark grinned. "I applied for a job as a derrickman."

The person who works on a derrick suspended above the rig floor, manhandling the drill pipe. Audrey had carefully compartmentalised away all the bad things that could happen to someone on a rig. Fires, fatigue, machinery, falls, being struck by debris, drowning, exposure to toxic chemicals, burns, helicopter crashes, electrocution, head and brain and back injury, muscle strain from heavy lifting and repetitive motions. And now her husband had applied for a job that meant he would be up so high, the mere thought of it made her palms sweat.

"Why did you do that?"

Mark's lips pressed tight. The night was going to go downhill quickly if she didn't say something positive. "I mean, I didn't realise you were thinking about changing."

"Well, to be honest, I didn't think I had a shot, but they told me today that I got it." Mark's eyes brimmed with excitement. "It's more money, and I report directly to the driller, which is huge. They're going to pay for the training as well. No more cleaning the drill floor and equipment. I'll get to monitor and maintain procedures of the well operations."

Audrey didn't know whether to feel terrified, excited about the extra money, or annoyed they hadn't discussed it.

Mark took both her hands. "This is a big promotion. Who knows where it could lead?"

She had to say something but was lost for words, so she leaned over and kissed him. "Congratulations."

An Asian man with an intelligent face in his late fifties looked over and smiled. He wasn't taking part in the conversation with the rest of his group. Audrey smiled back, but it was going to get weird if he didn't say something or turn back to his group.

"My wife doesn't like beer, so it's nice to see a couple enjoying one together."

Not normally that social with strangers, Mark extended his hand. "I'm Mark. And this is my wife, Audrey. It's our anniversary, so we're celebrating. Oh, and my promotion."

The two men shook hands.

"Lixin. They make very good beer."

Mark nodded. "I agree. Are you a regular?"

Lixin: "I come here sometimes, but I have a store in Mordialloc. Sally is my sales rep. We're all very upset about her disappearance."

Momentarily confused, Mark looked at Audrey. "She's the lady who went missing at the weekend. The one I was telling you about earlier."

Due to the beer or tiredness or a lack of interest, Mark didn't appear to make the connection. "Oh, right. I hope she turns up."

Lixin sighed. "Best sales rep they've got. Lucas is the brains behind the beer and Trish the business head, but it was Sally who saw the potential for a daily drinker and took their sales through the roof. It's one of theirs and our biggest sellers. They ran a piece on the news tonight asking about her date and if anyone knows who he is."

Audrey hadn't seen the news, but this was too good an opportunity to pass up. "Did Sally ever mention any problems at work or that she might want to leave?"

Mark frowned. Sensing Audrey had entered work mode, he excused himself. "Need to head to the gents."

The other men were listening now.

A man with a ruddy face and glassy eyes lowered his voice. "We're Sal's customers as well. They make great beer, but they're always running out of bloody stock. Sal was screaming for a database to record all the customer information, but the owners wouldn't have a bar of it. Apparently, one of them had a sales rep steal all their information at a previous company or some rubbish."

Sally wouldn't be the first person to ask her employer for something and not get it.

"I bet that was upsetting and made it difficult to do her job," said Audrey.

"You better believe it. She and Lucas fought like cats and dogs about it. If you ask me, this 'new platform' was never coming." Ruddy-face had a bit to get off his chest.

How heated did things get? "When you say fought…"

"I mean fought. Sal was in tears one day."

Lucas didn't seem like the type to push anyone to tears. Trish, yes, but not Lucas, although Audrey had met him only once, briefly.

"Come on," said Lixin, frowning at his friend. "Let's not make disparaging remarks. Time to make a move."

He looked at Audrey. "I'm driving, which is just as well. Enjoy your evening."

The men left as Mark arrived back at the table. "Sorry. That was too good an opportunity. Sally went missing after a date with a mystery man in Mornington last Friday. This woman is so routine that within hours her friends had organised a search for her. There's no evidence she was unhappy — quite the contrary. It wasn't why I picked here, for what it's worth."

Mark finished his IPA and picked up the ale. The wind could blow either way, so she was relieved when he finally asked, "Do they know who her date was?"

This was what she was looking for earlier. A little interest.

"No one knows who he was or how she met him. He even paid cash at the restaurant."

Mark scoffed. "Who the hell pays cash? Maybe for a coffee, but not a meal."

The earlier irritation melted away. Did she want someone in her family to show some interest in her work? Josh only asked the occasional question, and Beth was outright hostile, thinking her mother had settled, and not aimed high enough.

"That's what I think. Someone who doesn't want to be identified." She gestured to where the men had been seated. "But the fact that she argued with her boss is new to me. I was here earlier, and the owners were arguing over something as well. What if she threatened to leave?"

Mark's brow wrinkled. "And what, they bumped her off? It's beer, not international security secrets."

Hearing it out loud, it did sound ridiculous, but maybe they weren't one big happy family after all.

"Anyway, cheers to us," she said, getting things back to their anniversary.

"To us," said Mark.

They clinked glasses and each took a sip. Mark took both of Audrey's hands in hers. He was the more tactile one. It wasn't that Audrey didn't like hugs or kisses, or hand-holding; she did. But it didn't always occur to her to initiate. With their hands linked like puzzle pieces meant to connect and be inseparable once joined, she smiled. It was good to have him back.

Two hours later, Mark was sleeping soundly, judging by the purring coming from his side of the bed. Audrey had been staring at the ceiling for almost an hour. She had listened to a podcast and tried counting, but sleep wasn't coming.

Mark had sleeping pills, but the only time she had taken one, it made her like a zombie the next day. What was keeping her awake wasn't trying to locate Sally, or the news that she and Lucas had fought, but what was in the shed. Cath's team would have checked inside, but they would look for Sally, not clues to her inner world. Would Bill let her rummage through his daughter's belongings? Even with Sally missing, she doubted it.

In the initial stages of an investigation, it was important to act fast because memories faded. The first two days were when investigators usually had the best chance of following up on leads quickly. After the seventy-two-hour mark, though, progress typically slowed, and it became more challenging. Was the clue to Sally's whereabouts in that shed?

Audrey had the code to the key safe. Getting the keys and looking in the shed would be easy. But what if someone saw her? She could explain she was helping the family. Technically, it was breaking and entering, but only the shed.

She listened to Mark breathe next to her and closed her eyes. She was being impatient. Sleep would come. Or would it? She imagined each story she solved as a fragment. A tiny piece of herself being put back together. One day all the parts would come together. Jack, Aro Chol, and hopefully Sally Child. They would all heal the broken part of her that had come back to the place she never wanted to: Bennington.

The room was dark as Audrey shuffled to the en suite. A towel hung on the corner of the door, preventing it from closing entirely. She moved differently when Mark was here. Quiet, stealthy. On her own, she banged about and often put the bedside light on.

She preferred being able to move about freely, and while the logical solution was separate bedrooms, the idea had never taken flight. She enjoyed having him next to her, especially on nights she couldn't sleep and could extend her hand to hold his. The midnight ninja moves were a small price to pay.

Grabbing her phone, she unlocked the screen. Zero, nine, one, two. Was she really doing this? Carefully, she dressed and tiptoed outside.

16

The lawn was soft underfoot as she walked to the shed. Taking out the keys, her hands trembled slightly, but her mind was calm and focused. The first key didn't fit, or the second. The third did, and the padlock clicked open.

Quietly, she slid the handle open. Using the phone's light, she scanned the roof and walls. No Huntsmen spiders. On the ground were a hand mower, rake, and a small box of tools. On a shelf were two clear plastic tubs. One contained clothes, the second books and paperwork.

She removed the tub of papers and placed it outside on the grass. Inside were novels by well-known authors like Liane Moriarty and Nora Roberts. The selection looked like a bestsellers shelf at any mainstream bookshop. But no titles that gave any insights into Sally's inner world.

She spotted a final-year schoolbook. For some people, it held enormous sentimental value, since it represented the end of their academic journey and the beginning of a new chapter in their lives. There was an address from the principal, a speech from the previous year's dux, and then photos of each student in alphabetical order.

She found Sally quickly in a photo of a group of students at a sports day, grinning. Fresh-faced, and with an eager smile, she had changed little in the following years. The rest of the pages were class photos. Sally was in the middle row, once again smiling at the camera.

Audrey flicked through the remaining pages, growing more and more disappointed. Her own yearbook was full of high school mementos, notes, and autographs, handwritten notes and dog-eared pages, unlike Sally's, which was in pristine condition. What did that say about her? That she liked her things unmarred. That there were no significant memories from school? Or did she loathe school and couldn't wait to leave?

A person's high school experience was often a poor indicator of how the trajectory of their lives would go. Audrey had done well academically, and yet here she was working on a local newspaper, rummaging around in the shed of a missing woman, when she should be home sleeping next to her husband. But if Sally's high school years weren't good ones, why keep the book at all?

She took down the second tub. Inside were a few tops and jumpers. Nothing of interest. The answer wasn't in Sally's shed, but at least she knew. It was some consolation. It was time to leave. She put the tub back and slid the shed handle closed.

She placed the keys back in the safe as a car pulled up out front. She froze, her mouth suddenly dry. Had someone seen her? Footsteps came closer. Now what? Stay put and hope they went inside. But what if they came to the key safe? She sprinted down the side of the house, across the lawn, and hid behind the shed.

After several agonising seconds, a rattle came from the side of the house. Someone was at the key safe. Had Bill come back for something? He and Olive were the only ones who knew the code. Any trust developed with the couple would be gone if they found her. Or had Sally finally come home? She waited, listening to the footsteps cross the porch. Men had a more pronounced heel strike than women. It was a man, but who?

She waited for the lights inside to flick on. She could dash up the side of the house before they saw her and out to her car. But the lights didn't turn on. Instead, a torch beam snaked along the hallway into the kitchen. It paused and then disappeared back up the hall, only to reappear moments later. She waited, unsure and now scared. The torch made one last journey down the corridor before the front door closed and footsteps headed across the porch. The key safe rattled, the sound of the footsteps fading as the intruder walked away.

There was a chance she could still see who it was. Hurrying across the lawn and down the sideway, she made it to the corner of the house as a car engine started. She knew the distinct sound once described as evil Wookies.

It was a Volkswagen Beetle. She made it out the front as the Beetle drove away. Why was someone who knew about the key safe in Sally's house without the lights on? A thought circled. Olive had told Audrey the code, so who else had she blurted it out to? Were they helping themselves to valuables before Sally returned? A chill ran up her spine. Or was it Sally's mystery date looking for something?

She should call Cath Maguire, but to tell her what? That she was driving past Sally's house when she spotted someone inside with a torch? Then what? If she saw someone inside, she must have seen them coming out.

The litany of questions from Cath would be exhausting. For now, she had to keep this to herself and find out if anyone in Sally's circle drove a VW.

17

Audrey closed the front door and walked into the kitchen. She was surprised to find Beth in her PJs at the sink. "You're up late?"

Beth finished filling her glass. "I couldn't sleep." She turned the tap off. "How was your night?"

There was an edge to her question, which wasn't unusual. Beth's judgemental tone was a trademark, but today there was something else, some new and unfamiliar element that seemed to fill the air between them.

"Good. Your father enjoyed his tasting paddle."

Beth glared at her. "Where have you been?"

There was no mistaking the accusatory tone this time.

"I had to do something for work," said Audrey.

"Now? You work for a local newspaper, Mum."

She bristled at the not-so-subtle insult that Audrey's work wasn't proper journalism. She tried to explain. "Sometimes I have to follow a lead." But the way Beth looked at her made it clear that she didn't believe her.

"Is everything all right with you and Dad?"

This was unexpected. "Yes. Why are you asking me that?"

"You were gone most of yesterday, and now you're sneaking out at night."

Where was this coming from? "I'm helping investigate…"

"If you're having an affair, you can tell me. Heaps of kids' parents are getting a divorce."

This wasn't the first time Beth had accused her of this. Both times, the timing aligned with work, but her accusations were disturbing.

Audrey didn't know if she was shocked more about Beth's comments or the cavalier way that she said it. "I can assure you I'm not. If you must know, I was at the search for Sally Child. The woman who went on a date Friday and hasn't been seen since. It's kind of time-critical."

Audrey hoped her tone conveyed sufficient gravitas to put her daughter back in her place.

Anything Audrey told Beth could end up being broadcasted to her friends. "Yesterday I was with Donna at the search, if you would like to check, and tonight I had to call past a person of interest's house to check something. And no, I can't tell you any more than that."

Beth's shoulders sagged. Was she relieved?

"Did you really think I was having an affair?"

Beth looked at Audrey's clothes. "Well, it would be kind of weird if you didn't dress up at least a bit."

Audrey looked down at her outfit. Fair point. She grabbed her daughter playfully. Beth smiled, but something had made her say that.

Like any parent, she wanted to be a good role model for things like how to behave or make difficult decisions and how important friends were.

But she also wanted to provide a good example of a loving relationship. She felt confident the kids saw their parents as having a stable marriage. She wasn't so sure about the loving bit and made a mental note to hug Mark more in front of the children.

"Your father and I are not perfect, but we're okay. You don't get two Christmases any time soon."

Audrey held Beth, not wanting to let go. The hugs became more and more sparse the older they got. "Please don't tell your father, though. He might not be impressed that I snuck out for work at this time of night."

Beth side-eyed her. "Fine." She unpeeled herself from Audrey's grasp. "So, she disappeared?"

Most of the time, Beth was bored with her mother's line of work. Audrey liked it when she showed some interest.

"That's right. We think they may have walked down to the beach after dinner. Her car is parked in Mornington, so it appears she never made it back there."

Beth sat on a stool. "Was this their first date?"

Audrey sat next to her. "We believe so. Her date paid cash, and there was no CCTV footage of them. It's like she's vanished into thin air."

Beth thought about this. "Maybe they went to her place to pick up some things and then headed to his place. Although it's weird they didn't stay at her place."

She was right. If things were going well, why drive to someone else's place when they could have privacy at Sally's? But if they had gone to his house, Sally struck Audrey as the type who would pack a toiletry bag, and the blue toiletry bag was in Sally's bathroom. She could have another. "That's possible, but it doesn't explain why no one has seen her since. It's very out of character that she hasn't contacted someone."

Beth's face lit up, reminding her of Donna when she had an idea. "What if her date dropped her home because she'd had a few drinks and didn't want to drive, and someone followed them? And if they knew she lived on her own... I'd be looking at everyone who knew Sally lived on her own."

"That could be staff from hundreds of bottle shops, her family and friends, or anyone following her social media."

Or was it someone closer to home. Gavin?

"You really need to find her date. Go to TV, Mum."

The news had already run one piece on Sally. Audrey wasn't sure if there would be any interest in another piece unless there was some development.

Beth was excited, pupils dilated; her eyes appeared larger. "We did this in media studies. You need a story that really tugs at the heartstrings about her parents and friends," she said, sounding too detached for Audrey's taste. But she had a point. A heartfelt piece featuring Bill and Olive by a journalist with a huge following might help move things along. Beth's excitement faded. "Except you don't do TV."

There it was again. Her daughter's disappointment in her profession. Audrey wasn't a TV reporter, but she knew someone who was. It meant asking her nemesis, TV reporter Cam Andrews, for help. She would have to clear it with Cath and Eve, and of course Bill and Olive, but Sally was running out of time, and right now it felt like the best option. It must have shown.

Beth looked pleased with herself. "You're welcome."

Audrey looked at her intelligent daughter. "Please don't ever start dating."

Beth's cheeks blushed. Was there something special already? "I have to one day. Oh, there's a group of us going to Mexican tomorrow night for Cecile's birthday. She asked me to stay over, so I'll take my stuff and go straight there from school."

Cecile's family worked long hours in their food wholesale business, which paid for the enormous cliffside house they rarely had time to enjoy. The girls had been friends for years and stepped up their friendship since things cooled a little with her former best friend Amy after the Aro Chol case. Midweek sleepovers were normally not allowed, but this was a special occasion. But with Sally Child's attacker still out there, something about her daughter being out bothered her.

"Fine. But go to the restaurant and then straight back to Cecile's. No wandering around."

Beth's head recoiled. "A girl should be able to go out without expecting anything to happen to her, Mum. I'm not living my life because of a few creeps, but don't worry, I'll be careful."

Beth kissed her goodnight and left. She was right. A woman should be able to go for a night out and expect to come home safely. Unfortunately, that didn't always happen.

18

Silence. She'd drifted off again. How long was she asleep this time? Hours? Days? Her head pounded. Water. Then came the sinking realisation hit, she had none. Her lips were cracked, and her tongue felt like a dead lizard on the floor of her mouth. Even her eyelids felt dry, making it hard to blink. She tried to adjust to the complete lack of light but saw nothing but blackness.

"Help," she said to the darkness.

Her voice was gruff and raspy, like a smoker with a hint of broken glass and sandpaper. She tried again, but this time it was even more feeble and painful.

Every part of her body throbbed; all the effort of keeping her limbs moving had been undone. She turned her head and winced. Sharp pain ricocheted in her skull then pulsed through her neck, arms, back, and through her thighs. But she had to move. It would only get worse if she didn't. Placing her hands on the bottom of the barrel, she tilted to one side. Every joint in her body hurt. Her bones felt like they were grinding together.

What would Leo, her physiotherapist, say? Leo, with his horsey teeth and cheery smile. Leo, who fixed her shoulder when she fell exiting the chairlift at Mt Hotham. She could hear him now. "Come on, Sal. Someone trapped you in a barrel!" People wouldn't believe it.

She was going to get mileage out of this one, provided she got to tell everyone. Provided they were looking for her. Oh, how she wanted Leo to fix her now.

Was this her fault? She knew people made fun of her. The fact that she was so routine. Where's the spontaneity? Go nuts, Sal. Try something different. But she didn't like going crazy. Despite working for a company that sold alcohol, she wasn't much of a drinker. She enjoyed waking clear-headed and not wasting the day. Routine calmed her. It gave her a sense of control over the day. She was fine with an occasional surprise.

You couldn't control everything, but she preferred to know what her day would look like. What if everyone thought routine Sally was finally doing something spontaneous? Let's leave the girl alone. God, she hoped not.

Her mother was desperate for her to meet someone and not be alone. She owned her home and earned a good living, had an appropriate superannuation balance, but none of that seemed to matter unless Sally had a husband. It was infuriating at times, and yet a tiny part of her wanted to bring someone special to her mother while she recognised her. What if Craig, and Rick, and her parents, all thought Sally was with him? The sinking feeling was back. No. She couldn't think like that.

Tears streamed down her face, despite it being moisture she couldn't afford to lose. She sniffed and pictured them walking along the Esplanade. His hands were smooth and belonged to someone who took care of himself. She liked that. Most men had dry hands, like holding old leather.

She could see him sitting next to her with her parents. The conversation flowed easily. Did he try to call her the next day, and when she didn't respond, what if he thought she wasn't interested? No. No. No. She was interested. She had to get out of here to tell him how she felt.

Think. The house on the Esplanade. They were standing side by side, looking at it. They walked to and from Mills Beach. She only had one glass of wine, so why couldn't she remember anything after the beach? There had to be an explanation. Replaying their meal, she remembered going to the bathroom. Sometime between the entrée and mains. There was a queue because the restaurant was busy. Did something happen while she was gone?

Men who drugged their dates often wanted sex. Moving around, it didn't feel like she'd had sex. She wouldn't have slept with him that night, but it wouldn't be long. He must have known, seen it in her eyes. But what if he was one of those types who couldn't wait? Did he have his way and not want to face the repercussions? Was he the one who put her here? She gasped.

Who goes walking with a man they just met along a deserted beach? One who paid cash. It made him interesting but was it to hide his tracks. So no one could trace him? Was she that desperate to find someone to love? It appeared so.

Pathetic.

The search for love had turned her into a fool. It had made her forget everything she knew about how to stay safe in the world. She was stuck in a barrel because she wasn't smart or sensible. How could she be so stupid?

She wasn't a religious person, but if she survived, she would do things differently. So much time spent being scared of things and clinging to the hope a man would choose her to love. She wanted to be a mother, but there were other ways to make that happen. Technology was on her side. She knew women who had successfully managed it. She would keep herself open to love, but if it didn't happen, she would push on regardless. It was a pity she didn't feel that way about Gavin. She'd seen the way he looked at her, and her parents liked him, but it wasn't there. Craig and Rick could be the significant men in her child's life, and Gavin, if he wanted to. They could all be surrogate uncles of sorts. All she had to do was get out of here, and all that could happen.

The brewery used old wine and spirits barrels. At one point, Lucas and Trish had considered making their own. A Frenchman even came to see them and told them how they used oaks planks from forests in France and seasoned them in the open for three years. No glue or fixing was used, but the barrel's strength depended on the accuracy of construction. Lucas liked the idea of placing the barrels over burners to soften the wood and toast it and installing a pulley system to tighten the staves before a last ring was placed on the bottom. If only the equipment hadn't been so expensive. Sally smelt the wood. There was no scent of wine or beer. Barrels needed to be kept full and stored wet. If not, they became used up or "neutral" after four to six years. The older barrels developed leakage. Filled with rage, she smashed both sides of the barrel with her elbows. The pain was excruciating, but there was no mistaking the sound. A tiny split.

At most, a sliver, but enough to let in a smell. What was it? Ammonia and rotting meat. It was the same horrible, sweet, sickly smell she knew from her childhood, from the chicken farm.

Was she in the shed at their old house? Her aunt had bought the property before she died. They were excited to have a holiday home, but the idea vanished the moment they stepped out of the car. The smell clawing its way into the back of your throat. Her father hurried them inside, where it was bearable. But he had sold the place. So where was she now?

Her hands followed the seams of each panel, looking for the split. Then she felt it. Not the split, but something on her right hand. Bringing her fingers to her lips, there was no mistaking it: water.

19

T uesday

Audrey stood in reception at the Eliza James aged care home for the second time that week, trying to ignore the tiny voice telling her this was a bad idea. She hadn't envisaged collaborating with Cam Andrews again, but here she was. Cam was a TV reporter for Melbourne's southeast with an uncanny knack for being on the scene early.

If not for four men left clinging to a large cooler box and a single life jacket in the dark after their boat sank, he would have been covering Sally Child's disappearance. Abrasive and with a unique, inflammatory style of reporting, Cam had a huge following of involved supporters who liked to do everything from commenting on social media to helping solve crimes.

Their last encounter was after the body of Sudanese teenager Aro Chol was discovered at the foot of Chilton Hill. They had taken opposing sides from the outset but ended up not so far away. The only positive to having him involved was that if Cam's network got behind a story, someone might come forward who knew something or knew who Sally's date was. Audrey had to remind herself this wasn't about her.

Being a political animal, Eve was immediately on board with the idea. Collaborating with other media organisations could only benefit both parties in the long term. Nothing else mattered to Audrey except preventing Sally Child's face from appearing on the missing persons poster at local police stations, along with all the other lost souls waiting to be found. A brief mention on TV, Audrey's pieces in the *Gazette*, and Donna's update on social media had failed to get Sally's date to come forward. But somebody knew something. It was time to shake the carpet and see what slithered out, and there was no better way than with the snake walking towards her.

"Place is like a bloody resort. Bet it costs a bomb," said Cam, taking in the luxurious surroundings.

Audrey gave a tight smile, acknowledging both Cam and his cameraman, who was more concerned with managing his equipment. "They live around the corner, so follow me."

On the way, Audrey laid out the ground rules. "If there are questions they don't like, Sally's father Bill is going to give me the sign, and you'll need to stop, or the interview is over. And don't forget her mum has dementia. I don't know if it's a good or bad day until we get there."

Cam's jaw hardened. "My mother had dementia. I know the signs."

Fair enough.

A bleary-eyed Bill was waiting at the door. She didn't expect he'd had much sleep. "Morning."

Cam shook Bill's hand. "Thanks for speaking with us." He had the good sense not to attempt small talk.

They followed Bill into the living room. Olive was wearing a pretty floral dress, makeup, and pumps and greeted both men warmly, looking alert. "Good morning."

It appeared to be a good day. But there was a brightness to her that didn't suit the occasion. Bill asked, "Where would you like us to sit?"

Cam assessed the room. "How about you both sit on the couch, and I'll sit opposite?"

Cam pulled a chair for himself into position while his cameraman set up behind him. His proximity to the couple made Audrey feel protective and a little uncomfortable. She positioned herself to the side with a direct line of sight to both of them in case.

Audrey heard a knock at the door. It was Cath Maguire. Cath knew about the interview, and managing the media was part of her role, but not a part Cath enjoyed. "Didn't expect to see you here."

"Came to see if there's any new information."

And to make sure Cam did nothing to hinder their investigation. The window in which most missing persons investigations went in one of two directions had now passed. But did Cath's attendance mean they had little to go on? Despite this, Audrey was pleased to see her. Her presence would make sure Cam stayed in line.

Cam wasn't impressed but went with it.

Once the greetings were over, he waited for the signal from his cameraman and faced Olive and Bill. "Okay. Are we ready to start?"

"We are," said Bill, taking Olive's hand.

Cath looked at Audrey. Here we go.

Cam faced the elderly couple. "I'd like you to take us back to when you first discovered Sally was missing."

"When she didn't bring us coffee," said Olive, eager to please. "Every day she brings Bill a latte. He likes the little swirls they do on the top. And I like a cappuccino with lots of chocolate. The café is on the other side of the complex."

Bill cleared his throat, and Olive stopped talking. Was that a signal they had discussed between them?

Bill continued. "Our daughter is very good like that, so when she didn't arrive, we thought something was wrong and tried to call her. She didn't answer, and so we did a run over to her house."

Olive pursed her lips. "Her brother doesn't have a key because his last girlfriend wasn't very nice."

Olive's outburst made for great TV.

Bill frowned. "Can we cut that, please? That's private family information."

Cam was reluctant, but he wasn't an idiot. Declining would end the interview before it even got started. "Sure."

Bill's face was ashen as he recalled the morning. "When she wasn't at home, we started ringing around."

Cam continued. "Sally was last seen out for dinner at Armani's, a popular Italian restaurant in Mornington. The man she was with was described as average height, brown hair, no distinctive features, and he paid cash. They walked towards the Esplanade and turned right. There is no CCTV footage, so details about what happened after that are unknown."

"That's also my understanding," said Bill.

Audrey had an uneasy feeling about where he might go next. So did Cath, judging by the concerned look she gave Audrey.

"Does walking along a fairly deserted footpath with a man she only met seem out of character for Sally?"

Bill's jaw clenched. "Sally is a good judge of character. She must have trusted whoever she was with. Sally liked people. She worked in sales and got on with everybody, but she was no fool. If anything bothered her about the man she was with, she would have left and gone straight home."

Bill sat up and looked directly into the camera. "Whoever you are, please come forward. Or if anyone knows anything, please contact the police."

Cam had the sense not to pursue this line any further. "Sally's jacket was found at Bennington Park. Do you have any thoughts on how it got there?"

Bill would have considered the many possibilities, none of them good. "One theory is that someone robbed Sally and dumped her possessions later on. It happens quite a lot, so that may be what happened. Or she may have put it down and someone stole it. We'll need to ask her when she comes back."

Bill's confidence Sally would return was heartbreaking. Cath lowered her head. Every hour that passed made that less likely.

Cam continued. "Did you know if Sally had problems at work?"

Cath frowned. Audrey hadn't had a chance to tell Cath about what Lixin told her the previous night. But how did he know this already?

Bill sat up on high alert. "What do you mean, specifically?"

"Sally loved her job," said Olive. "Bill loves their beers, don't you?"

"Yes, they make a fine drop." Bill was keen to get back to Cam's question.

Cam asked again, "Was there anything at work that was bothering Sally? Did you notice anything different in the weeks before her disappearance?"

Bill looked torn, but he eventually said, "Sally loved her job, and her employers were good to her."

Cam's jaw hardened. He'd been hoping for more.

"She met Gavin there," said Olive.

"Gavin?" Sensing something, Cam sat up.

Audrey knew the look. Eager, enthusiastic, curious. Journalists were trained to keep an ear out for possibilities. At least the good ones were.

"He was her best friend at work. Actually, we thought they might get together because they get on so well."

Bill pointed his finger at the cameraman. "Cut that as well, please?"

There was no asking this time. Cam didn't respond.

But Olive wouldn't be stopped. "He was really keen on her. Such a pity she didn't feel the same way. He doesn't have much money, so we even talked about helping him out, didn't we, Bill? Gavin — if you're watching, we'd love to see you."

Olive was on a roll and had to be stopped. Cath stepped forward. Was she about to bring this to a halt?

"I think that might be all for today," said Bill, taking Olive's hands to stop her.

Olive looked straight at Bill. "Why hasn't he been to see us?"

"Olive! Stop!"

A heavy silence fell over the room. Cam turned to his cameraman and gestured for him to stop filming. Cath stepped back, no longer needing to intervene.

"Have you got enough?" asked Audrey, relieved the cameras had stopped rolling. Cam winced. Not really.

But then Olive turned to Bill with tears rolling down her face.

Cam gestured to his cameraman to get whatever she was about to say. "Sally will come home, won't she, Bill?"

Bill took both her hands. "Yes, love. Of course she will."

As Bill ushered Olive away, Cam turned to Audrey. "I do now."

Cath gestured for Audrey to speak with her outside. Once they were out of earshot, she said, "Troubles at work and helping Gavin out financially. Did you know anything about either of those?"

"First I've heard about them offering to help Gavin out financially."

Cath made a note. Did this mean they were going to take another look at Gavin?

"But last night Mark and I went to the brewery for our anniversary. One of Sally's customers said she and Lucas used to fight. Sounds like things got pretty heated. Sorry, I was going to call and tell you."

Cath's face tightened as she flipped over her notebook to check something. "He said they had a few run-ins over a database, but other than that it was one big happy family."

Audrey wasn't so sure. "According to her customer, Sally was in tears, so it sounds like things got pretty heated."

Cath looked thoughtful. "We'll speak to Lucas again. Anything else?"

Audrey shook her head. Not telling Cath about the late-night intruder at Sally's was hindering the investigation. It didn't sit well, but she had no choice.

"I better go and say goodbye," said Cath, walking inside.

Audrey's phone buzzed. She didn't recognise the number. "Hello, Audrey speaking."

A woman's voice came on the phone. "Oh, hi. My name's Di. I believe you want to speak to me." It was Sally's best friend. Well-spoken, her voice was filled with anxiety and despair. Fair enough. Her best friend had now been missing for three days, which would rattle anyone. "I can see you today if that suits?"

Audrey was keen to speak with Di. Best friends talked about the places they'd been and the places they wanted to go. They talked of the families they had built or wanted, their professions, and love in all its forms.

But best friends also kept confidences and typically told each other everything. Di didn't know Sally's date. Why? Had the two friends had a falling-out? Or was there another reason Sally kept his identity a secret? "I can be there in half an hour."

"I'll text you the address."

20

Di lived in a small brick home in the Boroughs in pristine condition. The small patch of lawn at the front was green and mowed. The weeded garden bed had been planted with Australian natives, the eaves freshly painted, and the front porch spotless and welcoming, with what looked like a new doormat. The two friends appeared to share a fondness for neatness.

Audrey pushed the doorbell.

"Coming," said a woman's voice through the speaker.

Di opened the door with a toddler on one hip. Everything about her screamed solid except for her eyes, which were red and blotchy. She'd been crying or hadn't slept, or a combination of the two.

"Hi, I'm Audrey. Thanks for seeing me."

Di opened the security door to let Audrey in. "Come in."

Audrey followed Di into a large kitchen/living room area at the back of the house, created via an extension at some point. The interior was as neat as the outside. "This is a lovely place."

Di placed her son on a mat in front of a set of blocks. "My husband, Charlie, is a builder, so he did it. It felt like such a box before. Can I get you anything to drink?"

"Just water, thanks."

"Please. Take a seat," said Di, gesturing to a timber dining table.

Di poured two glasses of water from a jug in the fridge and took a seat opposite her.

"It must have been hard to come home and find Sally was missing."

Tears poured down Di's cheeks. "Sorry. Excuse me." She removed a tissue from her sleeve and blew her nose. "I can't believe the one time I go away my best friend goes missing. People are saying she's run off with this guy she had a date with, but none of us who know her think that."

Neither did Audrey.

"Sal's not like that. She's also really careful. We always drive the other one to their car, and she wouldn't go home with a guy she just met."

Unless Sally and her date had been speaking for a while, and she no longer considered him a stranger. Emotions like love and infatuation can be powerful and cloud a person's judgement and decision-making abilities.

If Sally was infatuated with her date, she might have overlooked the warning signs or red flags that indicated he was dangerous. People often ignored their own intuition to pursue the object of their affection.

"If I went out without Charlie, she was always reminding me to park somewhere safe or make sure someone walked me back to my car. She was really serious about it."

If that was the case, did something happen back at her car? Or his car?

Audrey was keen to explore Beth's theory that her date had followed her home because she'd had a few drinks, and someone followed them. "Is it possible she had a few drinks and her date drove her home? It could explain why her car was where she left it."

Di shook her head. "Sal only ever has one drink because she figures men don't like women who don't drink. She had a hangover when we were eighteen and felt so bad, she'd never had one since. She's lucky if she finishes the glass."

So much for Beth's theory.

Di dabbed at her eyes. "I'll be honest, I was annoyed she hadn't told me about her date, but that's probably my own fault."

Oh.

"We used to tell each other everything, but the last time we spoke, I told her she was being too picky. There was always something wrong with every guy who asked her out. If I'd kept my big mouth shut, maybe she would have told me who he was."

Di was full of regret. If Sally didn't turn up, that would only grow worse.

Audrey was keen to get a feel for Sally's dating history. "Did Sally date often?"

Donna was a wise, astute dater who took precautions. Her ability to check a person's background and any inconsistencies before she agreed to meet further ensured her safety. But if Sally was new to dating, she might not be as worldly. Maybe too trusting?

"Sal's never had a problem being asked out. I mean, she's a friendly person. I tried to set her up with a friend of Charlie's who runs his own business, but she wasn't interested. She really wanted to meet someone her folks would be proud of. A professional or an academic."

"Was Charlie's friend okay with that?"

Di gave a tiny smile. "He met Rochelle, the love of his life, a week later. They're nuts about each other."

That was a dead end.

"Did Sally mention anyone else?"

Di looked thoughtful as she slipped back into the archives of her friend's dating history. "There was this one guy she was keen on a few months ago. I think his name started with an A. Aaron. Sorry, I can't remember his name. She met him at the gym. Sal was hoping it might become more, but then all of a sudden, she didn't want to talk about him. Sal could be full-on when she liked someone, so I figured he must have told her to get lost."

Di was smart. "Do you think something happened between them?"

Audrey shrugged. "I don't know. How long ago was this?"

"Not long. Maybe a month. I dropped it, but I could tell she was really disappointed. I think she really liked him."

Was this Sally's date? It was worth checking with Ash to see if he had noticed Sally flirting with anyone from the gym.

Audrey was keen to circle back to an earlier comment. "When you say Sally could be full-on, can you elaborate?"

Di's eyes grew wide. "I mean, full-on. She works out what restaurants they can go to, weekends away. I've told her to play it cool because it can scare guys off, but it's not her style. She's like that with everyone. Tell her you like something and next minute there's a courier at your door. She's a really good friend, you know."

Had Sally come on too strong with someone? Surely, they would have told her to back off before hurting her. An idea circled. Unless they had tried, and she didn't take the hint. What type of man would hurt a woman rather than tell her to leave them alone?

"Did you notice anything different about Sally in the months or weeks leading up to her disappearance? Anything that could speak to her mental state at the time she went missing?"

Di shook her head. "You know those people who are always there. Never miss a birthday or an important occasion. It's like they've got your back. Well, that's Sal. I'm like that too, which is why we get along, but she's next-level. So, no, I don't think she up and left."

The sinking feeling was back.

Audrey wanted to get Di's take on Gavin and his friendship with Sally. The fact that Olive considered giving him money.

"How well do you know Gavin?"

Di half rolled her eyes. "Well enough. Blind Freddy could see he was in love with Sal, but she was up-front with him. I've heard people saying they think he's the one who followed Sal, and when she was alone, he did something, but I can't see it. He lives near here, so I see him around a bit. He doesn't have many people in his life, so why would he do something to the one person who was there for him?"

Mild-mannered killers were scattered throughout history. Men, mostly, who one day snapped, shocking those who thought they knew them.

"I believe he's close to Sally's parents. Perhaps there was some financial gain to be had?"

Di shook her head. "You mean the will. Olive promises everyone a slice of it. I think I even got offered a piece once, but the only person who's getting their inheritance is Rick and Sally and Monash University, and if either of the two kids dies, their stake goes to Monash

University, not to the other sibling. Bill worked out a suitable amount for each child, and then the rest will fund the research he began. Sal was in charge of the wills and was a bit annoyed at the time, but she eventually understood."

"So, no one stands to gain financially if Sally goes missing?"

"Not except Monash University."

"Was Gavin aware of this?"

"I have no idea. Excuse me," said Di, going to attend to her child.

Audrey couldn't ask Gavin if their earlier interaction was anything to go by. He'd clam up the minute he saw her. He might respond better to Donna, but she was learning how to extract information from people. There was some finessing to do. Suddenly, the idea came to her: Stan. He could find common ground with most people and as a journalist was experienced at finding out information. She sent him a text. *Fancy a free beer?*

His response was fast. *Always.*

21

Audrey opened the door to the Bennington Pub with Stan and Donna in tow. It was the same after-work high-vis crowd from the other day, only there were more of them. Eve had agreed to let Donna leave early, provided she diverted the phone until the office closed, so Audrey didn't look conspicuous standing on her own.

Donna had been busy looking into the psychological profiles of men who would rather hurt a woman than tell her to leave them alone. "They often have a history of abusive behaviour and lack the emotional or psychological tools to manage their anger or frustration."

"Tell us something we don't know," said Stan, scanning the bar.

"They may also have a distorted view of relationships and believe they have the right to control or dominate their partner, even though in this instance Sally wasn't his partner, but you get the gist. Oh, and they struggle with their own insecurities related to power and control. Plus, the usual lack of empathy for others, blah blah."

Gavin struck Audrey as someone with a lot of insecurities. They didn't know about his family history, but the fact that he appeared to have adopted Sally's as his own spoke volumes. "Keep looking into Gavin and see what you can find."

Stan surveyed the crowd. "So, which one is our guy?"

Audrey spotted Rick holding court with a group of guys at a far table with his back to them. One man put his hand on Rick's shoulder to show support. Another handed him a drink.

Donna's eyes narrowed. "Looks like he's enjoying being the centre of attention?"

Audrey scanned the room. Gavin was at the end of the bar, nursing a beer, listening to a guy in his sixties with thick-rimmed glasses, a cardigan, and a glass of red wine to his left. A teacher after a hard day in the classroom, perhaps? It was hard to tell if Gavin was interested in the conversation, but his body was turned slightly away from the man, so maybe not.

Audrey turned to Stan. "He's the one in jeans and a grey hoodie at the end of the bar."

Stan clocked Gavin. "No time like the present."

Stan was a big man and moved through the crowd, easily positioning himself on Gavin's right. He said something to both men, and cardigan-man checked the time and left. Stan was now standing next to Gavin, both facing the bar. Audrey recognised the move. No eye contact. She used it when she wanted to get information from Josh. Stan signalled to the barman.

"Come on."

Audrey walked towards Gavin, making sure to keep out of his line of sight. She wanted to listen in without Gavin recognising her. They arrived as the barman placed Stan's beer in front of him.

Stan took a large gulp. "Oh, boy. Did I need that."

Gavin glanced at Stan but didn't respond.

Unperturbed, Stan continued. "What a day?"

Stan continued looking straight ahead. Audrey supported the lack of eye contact, but if Gavin didn't engage, or worse, motioned to leave, she hoped he had a plan B.

"I had a funeral today," said Stan, turning side-on to face Gavin. He was going to force the guy to interact whether he liked it or not.

Gavin nodded. It was only a small sign, but a sign nevertheless, that he had clocked Stan and heard what he said. Stan waited for him to make the next move.

Finally, he spoke. "Condolences."

Now that he had Gavin's attention, he took a sip and turned to face the bar. "It's fine. He was ninety-something and kind of a dick. Racist, tight with his money. I saw him kick a dog once."

Gavin looked at Stan. "So no great loss."

"Not really." Stan sipped his beer.

Audrey looked at a wide-eyed Donna and stifled a grin. It was an unusual way to build rapport. She was intrigued to hear the segue back to Sally.

"Anyway, how was your day?"

Audrey couldn't see Gavin's expression but could hear his response. "Had better."

Stan kept looking forward. "Sorry to hear that. Here's to a better one tomorrow." Audrey would ask about Gavin's bad day, but Stan's approach was more nuanced, even if the slow pace was excruciating. Stan raised his glass and Gavin clinked it. One more tiny step to build rapport.

Audrey busied herself on her phone for what felt like an eternity as Stan and Gavin nursed their beers in silence. It was unlikely two women would have stayed silent for that long.

Just as she was worried Stan had run out of conversation, he said, "But no matter how bad a day we've had, it can't be worse than the family of that woman who's gone missing. Sue, is it?"

"Sally," said Gavin. "She's a friend of mine, actually."

Stan feigned surprise. "Sorry to hear that, mate." He didn't make eye contact. "Know her well?"

Gavin nodded. "We're pretty close. We work together at Bennington Brewery."

Stan took his time and sipped his beer to give the news the gravitas it deserved. After what was apparently a suitable time, he said, "I hope she turns up."

"Yeah. Me too."

More silence.

"I've heard they make a good drop at the brewery. Probably should rectify that, being a local and all. Must be pretty hard for everyone at work."

"It's been rough. We all like her, you know."

And none more than you, thought Audrey, looking away from the barman, who glanced in their direction to see if she wanted a drink. It was a different employee today, thankfully.

A couple of girls had joined Rick and his friends. Rick hadn't seen her and Donna, and she was hoping he didn't until Stan was finished.

Stan continued. "The bit I don't get is why no one can seem to find this guy she had dinner with. Somebody must know him. It feels like he doesn't want to be found."

Gavin was quiet. Stan waited for him to respond.

"Sal's not the kind of person to run off, you know. She's close to her folks." Gavin glanced around to check who was listening. Audrey ducked, pretending to remove something from her handbag. "Her brother's a waste of space, so she does a lot for them."

"That's rough," said Stan. "Apart from all the emotional trauma, there's also the practical issue of who to leave everything to. Never got around to kids. My sister is gone, and her kids are a bunch of losers."

Audrey and Donna looked at one another, surprised. Stan had children. His sister was alive and well, and her son had been head-hunted by a large commercial engineering firm. Audrey hadn't realised he was such an accomplished liar.

"Donate it to charity, mate," offered Gavin.

"Suppose I could leave some for one of those charities that looks after us blokes, but I'd prefer most of it go to people I know. People who could do with a leg up," said Stan, pretending to consider his options. "Could have done with someone helping me when I was younger. Your folks alive?"

Gavin shook his head. "No. Long gone. There'll be no inheritance coming my way, that's for sure."

Stan made a final attempt. "Maybe someone else will leave you something."

"Nah. Fat chance of that. Hey, thanks for the beer, but time to go."
Gavin finished his beer and left.

Stan turned to face Audrey and Donna. "Holds his card close to his chest, but I don't think he's counting on being a beneficiary any time soon, and he seems pretty cut-up to me."

Audrey was disappointed. She had hoped Gavin was uncomfortable talking about Sally, but instead he seemed happy to tell a complete stranger how fond he was of her. It didn't explain why he didn't want to engage with Audrey the other day. Was it personal or the fact she was a journalist? But Stan had achieved what they came here to do. "That was really great."

Stan's chest puffed out. "Never thought I'd say it, but it's good to be back out in the field." He checked the time. "Is that all you need me for, ladies? I'm going to get home before Jan does for once. I'm watching a new series on Netflix. Might fit in an episode before she gets back."

"Thanks, Stan," said Audrey.

"Bye, old man," said Donna.

They watched him leave.

"He might stick with it for a while longer after all," said Donna.

Audrey hoped so. Stan's love of all things food, his no-nonsense style, and lack of desire to compete with her on the best stories made him the perfect colleague. She would miss him if he retired.

Rick slid out of his booth, reading something on his phone. He ran a hand over his head. Something was going on.

Donna followed her gaze. "Somebody's not happy."

Rick tapped a text back and waited. Whatever came back made him pale. His hands started clawing at his cheeks.

"Okay, he's really not happy."

Suddenly, he bolted outside. Audrey and Donna looked at one another and hurried after him. They made it outside as he climbed into a taxi, which sped off.

"What the hell was that about?" Donna asked.

"I have no idea, but something's going on. See what you can find out about Rick."

"On it. I got to go. Got a date."

If anyone could handle the perils of online dating, it was Donna, but Audrey felt protective. "Be careful."

Donna smiled. "Always. Oh, by the way. Eve liked my top-10 piece."

"Congratulations."

It wouldn't be long before the training wheels were off completely.

Donna left. Audrey checked the time. It was Sally's night at the gym. Mark wasn't expecting her home yet, so there was time to call into Next Level and see if Ash noticed Sally flirting with any members.

22

Audrey walked into Next Level Fitness and approached reception, where a guy in his twenties with a name tag that said Joe looked up and smiled.

"I was after Ash, if he's here."

"Sorry, he's doing a sign-up. He could be a while, but you're welcome to wait."

She didn't want to be here that long. Maybe Joe knew something? "Have you been here long?"

Joe shook his head. "Only a couple of weeks."

Maybe not.

Audrey could leave or use the opportunity to speak to a few members and perhaps find Sally's mystery friend herself. "I was hoping to have a look around. I'm thinking of joining."

Joe's eyes lit up. "I can give you a quick tour, but I need to look after the desk so might have to duck back."

"Sounds good."

Joe led her onto the floor, past the extensive range of various machines, asking polite but not too personal questions. Did she work nearby instead of where she worked. How often did she expect to come? Did she have a specific exercise goal? Enough to find out what membership would work best. He'd do well. But as they moved from the machines to weight benches, Audrey had the strange feeling she was being watched. She looked around but couldn't see anyone looking her way.

"Do you mind if I have a wander around by myself? Maybe chat to a few members if that's okay. I like to do my own research."

Joe blinked, momentarily confused by her request, and it briefly looked like it might be an issue until his mouth opened into a wide grin. "Not a problem. Come and see me when you're ready."

As Audrey wandered around, she sensed a couple of members looking over. A man with superhero blonde hair gave her the same entitled look that expensive private school boys used to flash at Bennington Station. She gave him a polite smile and kept moving. A married man on the rowing machine offered helpful information about the gym, his wedding ring catching the light as he gestured — friendly, but off-limits. Two younger men helping each other with weights didn't seem like Sally's type.

Then she spotted a man sitting on a weight bench, tapping his phone. As she approached, she could see it was a long text. No wedding ring either. He glanced up, but there was no offer to move or say when he was done. Not even a polite smile to acknowledge he had seen her.

Audrey took an instant dislike to him. "Hi. Sorry to bother you, but I'm thinking about joining the gym, and I wanted to know how you find the place."

The man bristled with annoyance and gestured to give him a second before pressing send and putting his phone away.

"What do you want to know?" He stood and had to be six foot six. There wasn't an ounce of fat on him, and his hair was thick and luscious, but he had mean, beady eyes. She couldn't imagine looking into those each morning. She'd learned how to spot the ones with women's issues. The ones who thought women should be seen and not heard. Women like Sally.

"I notice there's not a lot of women here."

Audrey watched closely for his response.

"Not tonight, but other nights there are. Is that a problem?" Suddenly, it felt like a stupid question.

"It's not really an issue. How do you find the staff and equipment?"

His phone buzzed. He tapped a text angrily. "I've had no issues."

Time to steer the conversation to Sally. "I hope you don't mind me asking, but is this the gym where Sally Child went missing?"

The man looked curious. "Yeah."

"I know she went missing after her date in Mornington, but sometimes I have to work late, so I wanted to know how safe this place is late at night." Audrey knew how to take care of herself. Always park in well-lit areas. Make sure a friend walks you to your car and drive them back to theirs. Never go to the beach with someone you just met.

Or would she? The reality was that if she had a great night and a few glasses of wine and felt like she could trust the person, she might do exactly that.

"I'm sure one of the guys who works here would walk you to your car. It's Bennington, after all."

"Did you ever speak to her? Sally?"

"A couple of times. She seemed pretty friendly, but I wouldn't say I know her." Still no emotion.

"How did you go, big fella?" said Joe, appearing behind them. "I hope you've put in a good word for us, Brian."

The man smiled at Joe and looked back at Audrey. "Actually, there is something wrong with this place. It's this idiot." The two mock-punched each other playfully. Once they'd finished their bonding moment, Joe said, "I've put a pack together for you."

"Great. Nice to meet you, Brian."

Brian gave her a dismissive wave but was already back to reading his phone. "Yeah. You too."

Audrey was following Joe back to reception when she spotted Olive and Bill on the TV.

"Can we turn that up? It's about Sally, the member that went missing."

Joe went looking for the remote.

Audrey watched without the sound. She would replay it at home with audio. Bill's face was a mask of worry and grief but also defiance and strength. He wasn't giving up on his daughter being found any time soon. She admired that,

Footage of Olive's hands clasped tightly in her lap, her knuckles white from the strain. A close-up of her face as tears welled in her eyes. Bill reached out and took one of Olive's hands in his own, their fingers entwined tightly. Cam and his team knew how to pull the heartstrings. She had to hope it worked.

Joe arrived with the remote, but the clip was finished. "Sorry. Someone moved it."

"That's okay." Audrey followed Joe back to reception and collected her pack as Ash said goodbye to a new member, judging by the way they both grinned.

Ash recognised her. "What brings you back here?"

"No word on Sally, I'm afraid," said Audrey.

Ash's face was full of concern. "I know. If there's anything we can do to help?"

"There is, actually. Sally's friend mentioned that she had a friend from here whose name starts with an A. Any idea who that might be? There's nothing wrong, but I'd like to speak with him if possible."

Ash surveyed the gym floor. "A? There are loads of members whose names start with A. We've got a few Tonys too."

Damn it. She'd been hoping the initial would lead them to the guy Sally was keen on. "Okay. If you think of anything, you've got my card."

Ash returned to work. Once again, Audrey had the feeling she was being watched. She looked around but saw no one.

23

From the change room, he watched Ash with the journalist. He'd seen her speaking with the detective at the park where he put Sally's jacket. There was a familiarity to their exchange, like they knew one another. Old friends, perhaps.

He hadn't planned on watching the search, but the temptation was too great. Now he understood why murderers attended their victims' funerals. He stood well away, so nobody saw him, but the feeling of power and control was like nothing he had experienced. He was the puppet master. Watching the strings dance, it felt like the world was at his fingertips, the sky and the stars his playthings, gravity itself at his beck and call. He'd never felt like this—and liked it.

She looked around the gym before leaving, with a gaze that seemed both curious and calculating. Good. He was glad she was gone. Something about her made him uneasy.

Ash would tell him who she was once he finished with the idiot who always overdid his weights. What would it feel like to be like Ash? So tolerant and content. You couldn't fake what Ash had. Was he jealous? Maybe. Had he ever felt truly content? Sure, there were odd moments, but they were few and far between. Until now. This had been one of the best weeks of his life. He wondered if even Ash had ever felt this good.

Ash finally finished with the idiot and walked towards him.

"I know her from somewhere." He tried to sound light and breezy but could hear the strain in his voice.

Ash looked at him. "She's from the *Gazette* and looking into Sally's disappearance. Ever notice her speaking with someone whose name started with A?"

He stifled a grin. The journalist was so off-base. "Not that I can think of. Why's that?"

Ash's face was full of concern. "Didn't say, but maybe they think it was her date. God, I hope she turns up. It's really weird."

He grimaced to feign sharing the sentiment, but Sally would never turn up again. She would never torture him again. He'd made sure of that.

But now Audrey Lord's presence tugged at him like an annoying child or animal. If he left, there was time to catch her. Record her number plate and licence to keep an eye out for it. "I need to be somewhere. Sorry, got to go."

He patted the bewildered instructor on the arm and rushed back to his locker, grabbed his things, and hurried outside.

The carpark ran for half a kilometre along the foreshore, so he'd need to move fast. Picking up the pace, he scanned cars to his left and right. It was quiet at night. The only source of light was the glow from the street lamps, which cast a ghostly flicker over the lot. She was here somewhere.

An engine started up ahead and to the right. He crossed to the other lane and saw it reversing. The driver had no choice but to pass him. The urge to see his potential opponent up close propelled his legs faster.

Removing his phone, he held it ready to capture both the car and number plate to study it later. The car drove towards him. His finger wavered over the phone camera, ready to take the shot.

Tinted windows made it hard to see who was driving, but as it came closer, he recognised a man from the gym. Where the hell was she? Spinning 360 degrees, he scanned the area, but she was gone. Damn it. Women. Why can't they leave things alone?

He walked slowly, eyes peeled for anything out of the ordinary. She was gone. Back at his car, he stopped and listened. The hum of traffic on the highway. Waves crashing against the shore, like a soothing lullaby.

He walked to the edge of the carpark overlooking the beach. The gentle, rhythmic rolling, followed by a muted crash of white foam—the sound of the tide ebbing and flowing—calmed him.

Would Audrey Lord let it go and move on to other stories or keep going like a dog with a bone and one day find him? That would be a mistake on her part.

24

Audrey walked through the front door and breathed a deep sigh of relief. It had been a long day at work, and all she wanted was to relax in the comfort of her own home. But as soon as she stepped inside, her heart sank.

The house was eerily quiet. Where was everyone? Beth was at Cecile's birthday, but where were the boys? She sent Mark a text. *Where are you?* She waited, but there was no response.

Unsettled, she walked around the house, searching for clues to where they had gone. Josh's school bag was on the floor of his room, a crumpled notebook on his desk.

How was he ever going to graduate with such poor organisational skills? It wasn't something she could solve now. She checked her bedroom. Mark's wallet and phone were gone. They were out, but where?

She was about to send a text when a car pulled into the driveway. Two car doors slammed, and Josh said something to his father and laughed. She was relieved; they were enjoying themselves. Audrey walked to the front door as it opened.

Josh was holding a takeaway bag. "Hey, Mum."

He leaned his face in so Audrey could kiss his cheek.

"Hi. What's for dinner?"

Mark smiled. "Japanese. I got you some sashimi and ende–whatever beans."

Audrey smiled. Did he muck that up on purpose? "Edamame."

She liked Japanese, so that was fine with her.

The three of them laughed and chatted for an hour. Josh looked so happy to have both his parents to himself without his dominant, eye-rolling sister nearby that Audrey was glad Beth was out as well.

Eventually, it was time for him to go; he'd organised to get online with friends.

"Not too late." Audrey had little control over what the kids did once she fell asleep but said it anyway.

Josh kissed her on the cheek and gave his father an awkward hug.

"Lights out at ten-thirty, buddy," said Mark.

"Okay."

Did he listen to Mark and ignore her? She let it go.

As Mark loaded the plates into the dishwasher and threw the rubbish in the bin, Audrey checked the time. The girls were staying at Cecile's and should be back there by now. She sent her a text. *Hope you're having a fun night. Home yet?* The dots danced. *Soon.*

"She doesn't give you much," said Audrey. "Not even an emoji to go with it."

Mark laughed. "Teenagers."

He only had to live with them half the time.

They both settled into reading. Mark a book on his iPad. Audrey finished catching up on emails from the day, but half an hour later Beth hadn't responded. It niggled like an itch that was difficult to ignore.

She sent another text and waited. Nothing. "Huh."

She dialled Cecile. No answer. Then Cecile's mother. No response there either.

Mark looked over. "Leave it. She's with her friends."

He was right, but it didn't stop the rising panic. They had bought Beth a new phone because the old one ran out of battery too fast. A quick *we're home* was all Audrey needed.

"Something feels wrong."

Mark looked up from the iPad and sighed. "Until she responds, we can't do anything. We have to wait."

Waiting had never come easy to Audrey. If Mark wasn't there, she would have called the restaurant and checked the girls had left and at what time. Based on the information, she would either give them enough time to get home or... would she really drive to Cecile's? Mark's parenting style was more lenient than hers, but was he right? Was it time to trust them more?

Audrey held the phone. "You're right."

Mark leaned over and took her hand. "She'll be fine."

The problem was that until she heard from Beth, they wouldn't know that.

"Turn the damn thing off."

There was no way that was happening, but she put it down.

Ten minutes later, the distinct Cookie Monster ringtone that Beth loved as a child rang. Audrey had been waiting like a tightly coiled spring, judging by the relief that came over her. What she wanted to say was *about time* and *where the hell have you been*. Instead, she took a deep breath, and, sounding as light as possible, said, "Hi."

"Mum. I need you to come and get me."

Something was wrong. Why was she whispering?

Audrey turned to face Mark. "What's happened?"

Mark put down his iPad.

"I'm at the bottom of Walkers Road."

What the hell were they doing there? But then another thought.

Audrey's voice went up. "Not on your own, I hope?"

"It's a long story, but there's this car..."

"A car, what, following you?"

Mark leaped up and grabbed his car keys.

"We're on our way but stay on the line. Can you give me a number?"

Beth whispered, "Near the top of the big hill. I'll get a house number."

If someone was prowling for their daughter, the safest option was to stay hidden. "Stay where you are. We'll find you."

Audrey hurried to Josh's door and opened it. His back was facing her while he played the game. "We have to go out for a few minutes. Back soon."

Josh waved and continued playing.

"Are you still there?" Audrey asked.

"Yes. Hurry, Mum. I'm scared."

Mark was already outside and had the car running.

"We're on our way."

25

M ark reversed out of the driveway and sped along their street. "She's near the top of the hill."

After what felt like an eternity but was only a few minutes, they turned into Walkers Road and drove to the top of the hill. Mark pulled over, and Audrey leaped out. "Beth!"

There was no response. Oh, God. She spun 360 degrees, looking for her. "Beth!"

The terror in her own voice frightened her.

"Beth!" she cried out again, her voice trembling with fear.

Audrey spun around in a circle again, searching for a sign of her daughter.

Mark had joined her by now, his voice straining with worry as he yelled Beth's name into the darkness. There was no response. They looked at one another. *Please, no.*

"Mum."

Audrey spun towards the sound of Beth's voice. Overwhelmed with relief, she rushed to her daughter and pulled her into a tight embrace. Beth was shaking, and Audrey felt tears streaming down her own face. She ushered Beth into the back seat and climbed in next to her.

"I was so scared," said Beth.

Mark climbed in and spun to face them. "What happened?"

Beth looked at both of them. "Clarice organised to meet up with this guy she knew. One of them had his licence and offered to drive us home."

Mark looked as unimpressed as Audrey was.

"You got in a car with a guy you don't know." His tone was angry, causing Beth to start crying. They waited until she composed herself.

"It wasn't like that. They were really nice, but he got a flat tyre on the highway, and it was going to take thirty minutes for someone to come, and Cecile's was only a fifteen-minute walk, so…"

Audrey was incredulous. "So you decided to walk home alone. On the Peninsula. On a night when no one is around? Why didn't you call an Uber?"

Audrey's voice rose.

"Mum. They're not coming for a trip that short."

Audrey never caught Ubers at night, but Donna did, so she would check that wasn't an excuse.

"Where are Cecile's parents?"

"They had a work thing on in the city," said Beth.

"Then why didn't you call me? I've told you to call if you're stuck."

"We didn't think it would be a problem," said Beth.

And it shouldn't be. But it was. The conversation about why Beth had ended up in this situation could wait until later.

"Then what happened?"

"We started walking back to Cecile's, and then this white car started following us. At first it was further back, but then it drove alongside us."

"Did you recognise the car?" Mark asked.

Beth shook her head. "It looked new. Four doors, like ours."

A sedan.

"We couldn't see who was inside. We started to walk faster, then started running, but it sped up."

Beth was a much faster runner than Cecile.

"Cecile was behind me, but then she said *this way* and disappeared down a track. By the time I stopped to follow her, the car was almost on top of me. I kind of freaked out and kept running."

Audrey had done the same thing as a teenager when a car full of boys chased her and two friends in the back streets of Bennington. The three girls had scattered like confetti at a wedding, the flight instinct taking over.

"I've never run so fast…"

Beth couldn't speak, the fear lodged in her throat. Neither had Audrey, fear propelling her legs to speeds she never thought possible and had never repeated since. That night, they all made it back to her friend's safely, albeit via different routes. Over the years, she had come to realise how lucky they were.

"The car was getting closer, so I ran into a garden and hid under a bush. Cecile was texting me, so I turned my phone to night shift in case they got out and started looking for me."

They. Now Mark's voice had risen.

"I couldn't see how many people were in the car."

Beth was right to think there could be more than one. One to drive and one to hold her daughter and take her god knows where. She tried to push down horrible images flooding her mind.

"You did the right thing."

Mark's voice was cold. "And did they? Come looking for you?"

Beth looked at her father and nodded. "I couldn't hear anything, so I came out the front and was about to run back to Cecile's when I saw the car. Its headlights were turned off, and it was rolling down the street."

Looking for their daughter.

Audrey gulped. She wanted Beth at home in her own bedroom tonight.

"We'll get your things from Cecile's, but you're staying at home tonight."

For once there was no arguing.

As they drove towards Cecile's, Beth nestled into her. Mark was angry. His jaw was clenched, his fists tight on the steering wheel, and the veins in his neck were visible. He would be annoyed at Beth but also himself. What if Audrey had turned her phone off? Would Beth have made her way back to Cecile's, or would the police be knocking on their door tomorrow morning? There was no need to tell him that.

Nothing she could say would make him feel worse than he already did.

Audrey went to dial Cath, but it was late. Instead, she dialled Bennington Police. Without a number plate, there wasn't much they could do, but an alert could be put out to look for a suspicious white sedan with tinted windows. Was it the same person who took Sally Child? Or another random weirdo who lucked upon two teenage girls in a dark street at night on their own.

26

Wednesday

Audrey and Donna followed Stan into the rear entrance of Bennington's latest café, a renovated weatherboard home on the beach side of the highway. She hadn't fallen asleep until sometime after two and desperately needed a coffee.

From the car park it didn't look like much, but inside it was gorgeous. Polished hardwood floorboards ran along the hallway and off to the sides, where former bedrooms provided private dining spaces for groups of mostly female retirees and local businesspeople. At the end of the hallway, the entrance had been converted into a reception area with tables for smaller groups.

Donna removed her jacket. "Good find, old man."

Audrey agreed, "Looks great."

Stan loved being the first to discover a new restaurant or café. Eve had once suggested he do reviews for the *Gazette*, but he wasn't interested. The last thing he wanted was disgruntled proprietors coming after him when he wrote that the health department should be called in. He didn't mind letting the proprietors know if a place was subpar.

Once seated and with their orders placed, Audrey poured three glasses of water as Donna took out her iPhone. Donna's morning had been spent scanning Rick's online presence. The only thing she had to show for it was a photo on Craig's Instagram of the two of them in front of a home brewing kit, each holding up a glass of beer.

She sat forward. "Rick's the family loser. He bounces around from one labourer job to another and doesn't have a lot of money, by the looks of it. His clothes look like they came out of the Vinnies bin. There's vintage, and then there's no money."

Stan glanced down at his clothes. "Some of these so-called IT billionaires dress casual these days. Whatever happened to a business suit?"

Donna sipped her water. "It's needlessly expensive. Most people wear fancy clothes to show how much they've got. They don't need to. Oh, and it prevents decision fatigue."

Stan looked confused. "Decision fatigue?"

"Choices become harder as the day goes on, causing your energy to get depleted, so sticking to the same look is one less thing to think about."

Stan looked at his standard shirt and pants, processing this. "And here was me thinking it was because I had my own unique sense of style."

Audrey smiled.

Donna continued. "But how I know he has no money is because when we were at the park after Sally's jacket was found, we went for coffee. I'd already said it was my shout, but most guys offer. Craig did, but Rick didn't."

Stan sat back, considering this. "He could be a tight-ass, but yes, that would be a reasonable assumption."

Stan glanced at Audrey. He was impressed with Donna's observations.

Donna lowered her voice. "He was telling me he'll need to get off the tools before he's too old. What if he got himself into some financial problems and someone was after him? It might explain why he bolted out of the pub last night."

Was Rick the one at Sally's the other night? Had he cajoled the number out of his mother and, knowing Sally wouldn't be there, gone looking for money or something he could sell? Audrey hadn't told her colleagues, but it was time she did.

She leaned in. "When I went to Sally's with Olive and Bill, there was a shed in the backyard. There wasn't time to look inside, so I called back that night to take a look."

Donna looked insulted. "And you're telling me that now?"

Stan's face was blank. "Go on."

It was hard to get a read on what he thought, but Audrey knew she could trust him not to say anything.

"There was nothing much in there—tools, a few books—but as I was leaving someone arrived. Another minute and I would have walked straight into them."

Donna's eyes grew wide. "What did you do?"

"I had no choice. I ran back into the backyard and waited for them to go. I thought Bill had come back for something, but whoever it was took the keys from the safe on the side of the house and then went inside using a torch."

Stan whistled. "They didn't turn the lights on?"

"No, which means they weren't meant to be there either."

Audrey let that sink in for a minute.

"Then what?" Donna said impatiently.

"I waited until they were done and put the key back and then hurried out to see if I could make out who it was, but I missed them."

Donna slumped back in the seat.

"They drove off in a VW Beetle. I recognised the engine."

The conversation paused as their drinks arrived.

"Double shot is for her," said Stan.

Donna waited until the server had left. "Rick drives a ute. He had to grab something out of it when we went for coffee."

"Gavin drives a white sedan," said Audrey.

"Unless he borrowed it?" said Stan.

That was a possibility.

"I'll see if I can find anyone in Sally's world that owns a VW," said Donna.

Audrey continued, "Do that, but I'd like to speak with Rick alone, without Craig or his parents and without giving him any warning I'm coming. I can't tell him about Sally's visitor, but I can say we saw him at the pub, and he seemed upset. Maybe he'll say something."

Stan sniffed. "How are you going to manage that?"

"I was thinking of a surprise visit to his work."

Audrey looked at Donna with her long black fingernails wrapped around her iPhone like the precious weapon it was. "Don't suppose you can find where he's working?"

Donna gave Audrey an *are you kidding* look, then tapped into her phone and scrolled. Her fingers splayed an image. More tapping, until she dialled a number.

Sitting upright and in a light and breezy tone she said, "Oh, hi. Rick left his lunch, and I wanted to drop it off. I forgot to ask where he's working today." Donna listened. "What number's that again? Great, thanks. Have a good day." Donna hung up. "He works for a local builder and is at 45 Rubin Street in the Boroughs today. You're welcome."

Stan looked at Audrey. "Remind me never to get on her bad side."

Donna pointed a black nail at Stan, smiling. "That's right, old man."

27

Rubin Street was a dump, with most homes long overdue for demolition. Audrey parked behind a half dozen utilities and a large skip full of rubbish from a home in the final throes of levelling. Sometimes it was easier to start again.

The blue sky from earlier was gone, and light rain now sprinkled. Melbourne and its four seasons in one day made life challenging at times. She searched for the small, pull-up umbrella Josh had used last and as usual hadn't put it back. The hood on her puffer jacket would need to do. She pulled the hood up and climbed out.

Up ahead was a man in his late twenties wearing shorts and a high-vis vest. Seemingly unperturbed by the weather, he was checking his phone, sipping his Thermos of coffee. Tradies never seemed to feel the cold, or perhaps they got used to it.

"Excuse me, I'm looking for Rick. I think he works here."

The man's face frowned. "Must be one of the new guys." He yelled, "Zipper!" to a man at the entrance of the block. "This lady's looking for Rick."

Zipper acknowledged he'd heard and yelled, "Rick. There's a chick here looking for you, mate."

Chick? Audrey left Thermos man and approached Zipper, expecting to see Rick make his way towards her. Instead, he hurried out of the block without glancing at her and took off in the other direction.

Zipper looked as bewildered as she was. "What the hell's he doing?"

There was no time to explain. Audrey hurried after Rick as the rain started to pelt down. Beth was always on at her for not wearing heels, but right now she was pleased she had her flat black boots on and broke into a jog.

She called, "Rick. It's Audrey from the *Gazette*," but the rain made it difficult to hear.

Rick turned left. Audrey had no idea where he was going and continued to follow him for another two blocks. It felt good to move, and she could feel her legs and breath settle into a rhythm. She was closing in and could tell he was tiring. Rick ducked left into a house. She slowed and stopped at the entrance. The only hiding spot was down the side of the garage. Poking his head out, he realised he'd been cornered and yelled, "I don't have your money."

Audrey removed her hood so he could recognise her. "Rick. It's Audrey from the *Gazette*."

Fear turned to confusion, then recognition and embarrassment.

"Shit. I thought you were someone else."

"I figured that," said Audrey, slowing her breath.

"What are you chasing after me for?"

"I'm not. I wanted to ask you a few questions. Who are you running away from, anyway?"

Rick put his hands on his head. "I owe some money and his daughter does the debt collecting. They're not nice people."

Was it the Millers, the Borough's most notorious crime family? "Name's not Miller, is it?"

Rick's head recoiled. "How the hell do you know that?"

Family matriarch Sharon Miller was the reason Audrey had left Bennington. "It was a long time ago, but our paths have crossed, unfortunately. I don't look a thing like Sharon Miller, though, so who does the debt collecting?"

Rick's eyes bulged in fear. "Briony." Audrey didn't know the name.

"She's about your height, so I thought it was her. She injects stuff into people who don't pay while one of her goons holds you down. I know a guy who's not right in the head after he got one of Briony's jabs."

Briony sounded like a real piece of work. Hopefully, Cath Maguire had this woman on the radar. Audrey would check.

"We saw you run out of the pub the other night."

All the joy left Rick's face. "Someone told me Briony was looking for me. That's enough to kill anyone's night."

The rain was easing but still falling. Rick looked like a sodden mess. "Can we walk and talk? I don't want them docking my pay."

Audrey wanted to get out of the rain, and no eye contact meant she'd get more out of him that way. "Sure."

Audrey hurried alongside Rick, who set a cracking pace.

"So, what did you want to ask me?"

How annoying was it to be considered the useless member of the family? How did it feel to be the only one not trusted to have a key to Sally's house? And did you break into your sister's house the other night?

"What Sally was like as a sister."

"You came out here in the rain to ask me that?"

"I've spoken to Craig and your parents, but you're her brother. I'm thinking you probably know her better than anyone."

Rick looked a little surprised, like he wasn't used to having his opinion valued. He wrapped his arms around himself like that would help prevent more rain from getting in. "Okay. Well, I suppose she's a pretty good sister as far as sisters go. Always remembers my birthday, buys me nice presents, and she used to help me out with a bit of money here and there. Not anymore, though."

Oh.

"She would, but I asked her to stop helping me. I need to stand on my own two feet, you know."

Audrey hadn't expected this. "Did that change things between you? The fact that she stopped helping you out financially?"

Rick shook his head. "Nah. Sometimes I get on the sauce and do stupid things. I'm not an alcoholic or nothing. I can go without it, but when I do, it's like fireworks in my brain. Like anything is possible."

Alcohol had that effect on lots of people.

"Don't always do things I'm proud of, so I told Sal and the folks not to give me money in case I'm having one of my..." Rick pretended to blow his head. He stopped and faced Audrey.

"Listen. I didn't hurt my sister. You think I want to look after my parents alone? No way. You're barking up the wrong tree."

Audrey hadn't considered the burden of being the only remaining child. Bill and Olive didn't need looking after. They had first-class care for when Olive deteriorated, which meant Bill didn't have to, as was often the case with home carers. But that didn't take into account the emotional support required by an only child.

Audrey wanted to make sure. "So, there was no resentment between you and Sally at all?"

Rick brushed the water off his face. "I'll be honest, sometimes she can piss me off. Sal's so by the book, you know. And man, if you say you're going to do something and you don't, she's really not happy. It's kind of what we all love and hate about her. Well, not hate, but you know what I mean. But I knew she was trying to help me, so it's hard to stay mad at someone who wants the best for you."

They turned the corner and were almost back at Rick's work. Rick had asked Sally not to help, but what about his best mate, Craig?

"How about Craig? You've been friends a long time." Audrey was curious why Craig let him hang out in the breeze with Briony after him.

Rick scoffed. "He's got no money. His bitch of an ex hits him up for anything she can to do with the kids. Told him not to marry her, but he wouldn't listen."

Rick's exes were on drugs, and he had the Millers after him. It wasn't surprising Craig didn't take advice from his friend.

"I know he'd help me if he could, but he can't."

The rain was easing up. Rick looked at the sky with a hopeful expression. He reminded Audrey of a friend's dog, a mutt, loveable but erratic, and a mess. Nevertheless, she was warming to him.

"Can't you ask your parents for a loan? If this Briony is danger-ous, it might be worth getting her off your back. The Millers can be very persistent."

Rick shook his head vigorously. "The only thing worse than Briony is the disapproving look my father gives me when he asks what

I've got myself into this time. If I can hold off for a few more days, I'll get paid, and then I can get Briony off my back."

Rick's phone pinged. Hands frozen, it took him several seconds to pry it out of his pocket. "It's Craig." His face grew angry. "Crying out loud. The brewery's putting on an event tonight for Sally like she's dead."

Audrey didn't keep notifications on and opened Facebook. The event's name was *Friends of Sally*. Tonight, 7:00 p.m.

"Tight-ass pricks probably want to make some money now their star sales rep's gone." Rick looked furious.

Audrey tried to put a positive spin on it. "It's a chance for everyone who knows Sally to come together. It might prompt someone to remember something."

Rick put his phone away. "You going to go?"

Mark was taking the kids to a movie. Audrey had planned to join them, but this was too good an opportunity. The kids wouldn't care, but Mark would. She'd organise something as a family at the weekend.

"I'd like to, if that's okay," said Audrey, treading carefully. "It might be helpful."

"Why not? Let's celebrate my missing sister and see what comes of it." And with that, Rick the loose cannon stormed back to work.

Audrey shared the event with Donna. Everyone from Sally's world in one place. This could be interesting.

28

"I can't see any VWs," said Donna as Audrey lapped the brewery carpark and then the surrounding streets. It was worth a shot but time to get inside.

Around two hundred people filled both the courtyard and interior.

"Good turnout." Donna smiled at a group of men in their late twenties who turned to look at her. She wore designer jeans, a silver-grey top, a black leather jacket, and stylish black boots with heels. Flawless makeup and hair. The perfect long black nails were a given.

Audrey had good skin and was in good health, but the next-level grooming skills of people like Donna had eluded her. Seeing someone well put together was something to be admired, and right now Donna had several admirers.

"Maybe I should start coming here," said Donna.

"Maybe." Audrey spotted one man looking at her. She wasn't interested but didn't mind the odd bit of attention.

"How do you want to do this?" Donna asked. "Divide and conquer or join forces?"

Audrey spotted Olive and Bill inside with another couple. The crowd inside was older, so it made sense to let Donna work outside. "I'll take the oldies inside. I'll let you handle out here, but," she gave a wry smile, "don't forget we're here to work."

"Yes, Mum," said Donna. "What about drinks?"

Audrey spotted Jake behind the bar. "I'll get them. Do you want the same one?"

"Better not. Knocked me for a six, so maybe an IPA."

Donna headed off to chat to the table of male admirers. The girl's confidence was inspiring.

Audrey stood at the far end of the bar and positioned herself so she could survey the entire room. Jake and another barman looked flustered as they served drinks to the thirsty crowd. This could take a few minutes, so she poured herself a glass of water from a jug.

"You made it," said Rick, looking better than their earlier encounter. Now in dry clothes and freshly shaved, his cologne took Audrey back to high school. But there was something else. The fear was gone.

"You seem better?" Audrey was curious about the turnaround.

Rick breathed out. "Boss gave me an advance, so the dogs are off me for now."

"That's good." Nobody wanted a Miller on their tail.

Jake spotted Audrey. "Hey. What are you having?"

"I'll have an IPA and a gin and tonic, please."

Audrey gestured to Rick.

"IPA thanks, pal." He turned to Audrey. "Thanks."

Audrey spotted Bill. His face was strained. In contrast, Olive was laughing and smiling, causing two men nearby, clearly not aware of her condition, to frown.

"How's Mum and Dad holding up?"

Rick's eyes were pools of distress as he leaned farther onto the bar. "Dad's not saying much, and Mum thinks Sal will be home any minute. Every time she says it makes me think it's less likely."

It had now been five days since Sally went missing. Rick's dismal outlook on his sister was warranted. Nevertheless, Audrey had come here to find anything that might help locate Sally and mourning her wasn't going to help anyone.

Audrey looked at the room of strangers. "I don't know many people here, so do you mind pointing out who's who?"

Rick turned around. "Okay. The folks you know. Craig, you know."

Craig stood in the corner, back from his interstate trip, chatting with a woman his age. His body language was stiff, and he didn't appear to be enjoying himself.

"Is that his wife?"

Rick scoffed. "Ex. No. That would mean she was socialising. No idea who that is. I think they just met, but doesn't look like he's having much fun, does it? I might need to rescue him."

Audrey followed along as Rick gestured to various groups around the room. Di with other friends of Sally's from school. Family friends. Maybe customers. She recognised Ash with a group of fit-looking women, presumably from the gym. The rest Rick didn't know. Audrey had once scrolled through Mark's Facebook page, realising she only knew about a third of the people in her husband's life. Where was Gavin? She was keen to get Rick's take on him.

"Do you know Sally's friend Gavin?"

"We all know Gavin," said Rick, imitating doe eyes. "Got the hots for Sal, even though she's told him she only wants to be friends."

Jake put their drinks down and pushed the terminal towards Audrey, who tapped her card. She waited for Jake to leave and, trying to sound as nonchalant as possible, said, "Gavin seems to get on well with your parents."

Rick's jaw clenched. She'd hit a nerve. Good. He took a large sip of beer, which he seemed to need.

"He goes with Sal sometimes to see them. Kind of weird if you ask me, but the guy doesn't have any family, so I think he's kind of adopted my folks as his own."

"Is he here tonight?"

Rick craned his neck to look around. "He was here before. Must be in the gents or out the back, managing stock. Knowing Lucas and Trish, they'll be making sure there's plenty available tonight."

Audrey noted the hint of bitterness. Sally was missing, but life and business went on. "I need to give my colleague her drink."

"All good. Catch you in a bit."

Rick clearly had no intention of moving from the bar.

Donna was in the courtyard, speaking to a cute guy in his late twenties. A flash of guilt crossed her face as Audrey approached. "This is Evan. He used to work here, in the warehouse."

Evan was handsome, with an intelligent face. "I used to, but now I work for Liquorland on the commercial team."

He seemed like a nice guy, and there was definitely chemistry between him and Donna. "Nice to meet you, Evan."

While Donna and Evan continued chatting, Audrey spotted Lucas on the other side of the courtyard, only half listening to a man talking about beer, by the way he kept referring to his glass.

Lucas's gaze was on a conversation going on nearby involving Lixin, the customer she had met the night she was here with Mark and Trish. Lixin looked upset about something. Was it business or something else? Trish took Lixin's arm and led him inside.

"Excuse me," said Audrey, hurrying inside. She briefly lost sight of them but then spotted Trish's hot-pink dress disappear around the corner near the barrels. The crowd thinned towards the end of the room, so she busied herself with her phone to look less suspicious and waited. She was too far away to listen in but could wait until they returned.

Several minutes later, Trish disappeared into the office, and Lixin walked past.

"Hi, Lixin. We met the other night."

It took a minute for him to recognise her. "Sorry. Yes. You were here with your husband."

"That's right. I thought I'd come along and support Sally's night when I heard she was still missing. Sally was your sales rep, wasn't she?"

His face was flushed, like he was trying to calm down.

"Is everything okay?" Audrey asked.

"Yes. Sorry." He took a deep breath. "There's been a few issues this week with Sally not being around. I'm trying to be understanding, but I've got a business to run."

Things weren't working well with Sally gone. The business had problems with stock control, and Sally was screaming for a database to manage things that never came. An idea circled.

"Lots of companies struggle when sales reps leave or go away. Take all that valuable IP with them." Audrey tapped her head, trying to sound light.

Lixin shook his head. "Not Sally. She kept detailed notes because she remembered everything. I once offered her a job to come and be my office manager. She laughed, but I was deadly serious."

Lixin's phone buzzed. "Sorry, but I've got to go."

It made sense that someone who liked detail and order would set up their own method of record-keeping. But where was the information now? Not in the back shed. The police had searched Sally's place. Perhaps they had found something.

Audrey stepped into the bathroom and dialled Cath. "Audrey. How can I help you?"

Cath's clipped, formal tone meant she was at work. Good. There were only so many times you could call someone after-hours, even if she was a friend. "Sally Child's computer. Did you find any customer files on there?"

"Hang on." There was a brief delay until Cath spoke. "There were a few general work files, but nothing relating to specific customers. Why's that?"

"Don't know yet. I'm at the brewery, and one of her customers mentioned she kept detailed records. I was wondering whether there was anything that looked interesting."

"Not that we found," said Cath.

"Any joy on the missing date?"

"No, but we're having a ball working through all the calls from women telling us to look at all the creeps they dated."

Audrey felt for Cath, but she had signed off on the interview as well, so she knew this was a possibility. There was still the matter of Gavin. "How did you get on with Gavin?"

"We took another look, but there's nothing there. Apparently he really likes dumplings." Fortunately, Cath didn't sound upset about the dead end. "I'll let you know if we hear anything."

"Okay."

If Sally's customer files weren't on her computer, where were they? On a USB or hard drive? Did this information have anything to do with her disappearance? If so, was that why someone was at Sally's the other night? The thought was unnerving. Was that black cat trying to warn her after all?

Audrey looked in the mirror and frowned. She needed a haircut. But slowly, another idea formed. What if the information was still there? Everyone who knew Sally was here tonight. There would never be a better time to look.

Audrey hurried back to Donna. She was clearly breaking up something between her and Evan, but it would have to wait.

"I need to get to Officeworks. I promised I'd grab Beth something, and they close soon."

Officeworks was a large stationary chain with a store around the corner that was open for another hour. It was all she could come up with for now.

Donna looked confused and disappointed. "Now? Okay. You're driving."

Audrey felt torn. If anyone saw them, they would both be in trouble, but she was going to need Donna's help. The faster they could get in and out of Sally's, the better. "Don't suppose you could come with me?"

Evan looked disappointed. "I've only had one drink, so I can drop you home."

"Sorry, but I need Donna to come with me," said Audrey.

Grateful she didn't have to spell out why, Donna took out a glossy black business card and handed it to Evan. "I'd love to continue this another time."

Evan's face lit up. He tucked the card carefully into his wallet. "That'd be great."

On the way out, Donna said, "This better be good."

"That's what I'm hoping."

29

He watched Audrey Lord and her cute friend leave. Why were they going so early? Was it something to do with the kids? He had no intention of speaking to her but was hoping to watch her for longer.

Keep your enemies close, they say. He'd been doing that. Her Facebook banner photo showed her husband and two kids in school uniforms. The husband was on Instagram. Lots of posts of meals on an oil rig. Did the idiot not consider he was announcing to the world that his family was often home alone?

He'd found the girl from her school uniform. She was sporty and bright, judging by photos on the school's Facebook page. Part of the swimming squad. Winning a history competition.

He never understood why parents allowed their kids' photos to be put online. He had no interest in children, but plenty of weirdos did. There was nothing online on the son, but he probably used a fun pseudonym.

The woman clearly aspired to more investigative work and now had her sights on finding out what happened to Sally Child. Why? Was it because Sally was a woman, or was that how it was with journalists? One day something captured their attention and then they were like a bloodhound on its trail. He hadn't seen a TV interview with Cam Andrews and his nut job supporters coming.

That rattled him. Overnight, Sally went from being a local to someone everyone knew. Suddenly everyone was talking about her. Had Sally done a runner with her mystery man? Did Sally's mystery date have something to do with her disappearance? Did she have mental health issues and simply vanish? Around thirty thousand people go missing in Australia every year. One every eighteen minutes. But now every nut job was on the lookout for Sally bloody Child. They would never find her, and certainly not after tomorrow.

He took a seat at the rear of the courtyard. People were enjoying the camaraderie of the night. Some were laughing. The first time he went to a funeral, he couldn't get over how the wake was like a party.

How could people be happy when they had just buried someone they loved? His mother explained that the wake was the opportunity to celebrate the person they knew. The time for grieving was when they got home.

This was Sally's wake, except none of them knew it. As he listened to the people nearby, there was the odd naysayer, but most people were hopeful she would come back. Fools.

As a boy he had learned to be a good listener. It was how he could tell when things were about to explode between his parents. He had learned to pinpoint the exact moment when things turned dark, right before the fighting and screaming began.

If he was quick and locked his door and put his headphones on, he could almost pretend it wasn't happening. Except for his mother's battered face, the following morning they were a normal family. He couldn't thank his father for much, but he had made him a good listener.

It wasn't all bad. Sometimes his father would tell his special bedtime story. Not the kinds of stories other kids had read to them. This story was about a woman who had slept with other men and was placed into a live tomb without any exits as punishment. His father explained that it was different from putting someone in a coffin, where they died of asphyxiation.

This person died from both starvation and dehydration. Two for one, as it were. He could see his father smile when he said that.

The first time he heard the story, he cried. It frightened him. Would he come home one day to find his mother gone? Buried somewhere never to be found. His father assured him he wouldn't touch his mother. While they had their problems, he couldn't live without her. He believed him.

But his father kept telling the story and over time creating characters to go with it. There was always a bad woman who tormented the long-suffering man who loved her. Over time, he too came to see that the women deserved what she got. For hours they talked about the type of tombs they could create.

Building walls. Bridge walls. Barrels. How the man got to enjoy the thought of her suffering for days, locked up in a special place only he knew about. And then his father died. Then his mother. But not the story.

Sometimes he would fantasise about creating a live tomb for the different women who made his life difficult. The ones who wanted more from him. The ones who saw the exterior and projected a version of life onto him that he didn't want and could never provide.

Some got so close, they made him feel like they were crawling down his throat to the dark part of himself even he didn't want to see. When that happened, he froze them out. Eventually they got the hint and left. They had no idea he was doing them a favour.

And then along came Sally Child with her upbeat, annoying presence. He loved the gym. Not a piece of Lycra in sight. They played music, but not too loud. It was clean and didn't stink of sweat and had ice-cold Gatorade in the fridge. It quickly became his home away from home. A place where he could relieve the tension that darted around his body like a wild current.

The combination of the workout and environment calmed him. Those were the nights he slept the best. For a brief, blissful few months, his life had been perfect. Until, of course, everything went to shit.

Sally had a great body, and she was soon all he could think about. At first, he thought he was falling for her. Then, that he was having an early midlife crisis. For weeks he couldn't work out why she bothered him so much. He was driving home from work one day when it finally came to him. But it wasn't purely attraction. It was her predictability that drew him. Same gym schedule, same route to work, same coffee run for her parents. She was like a lab rat running the same maze, making her the perfect target.

His father had always told him about his favourite victim in their special story. A woman so bright and hopeful that the man had no choice but to snuff the life out of her before her positivity suffocated him. Sally was just like that woman.

But neatly tucked away in the dark recesses of his mind for all those years, the urge crawled to the surface. It became all he could think about. His father's words rang in his head day and night. Why would someone kill a person with a weapon? It was over so quickly. Why deny yourself the pleasure of knowing that as each minute passed, the person was moving slowly towards death? Now unleashed, the urge wasn't going to go away until he did something to satisfy it.

Driving around looking for a suitable place, old bridges, tunnels, he began to lose hope. Until he overheard a conversation. After that the details fell into place.

No one could survive five days in a barrel. Sally was gone now. Savouring the deliciousness of the situation, he felt a rush of excitement.

He made his way through the crowd and into the men's. It was empty. Good. Closing his lips, he inhaled for a count of four, then exhaled for a count of eight. On the third cycle, the exhilaration subsided. A splash of cold water on his face helped. He stared in the mirror and smiled.

If only his father could see him now.

30

Audrey parked a few houses down from Sally's in case any nosy neighbours recognised her car. On the way, they had stopped off and bought a packet of plastic gloves. They would have a hard time explaining Donna's fingerprints if this became a murder investigation. She removed two sets and shoved them in her pocket.

"Follow me to the safe, and then I'll need you to provide some light while I get the keys."

"On it."

They hurried up the driveway and to the side of the house. Audrey tapped in the code. Zero, nine, one, two. It hadn't been changed, and the safe opened. Audrey closed the safe and hurried onto the porch towards the front door. The second key opened the front door. It was a relief to be inside.

The curtains in the living room were open. Lighting from the street provided enough to see the layout of the place.

"Smells nice," said Donna.

The scent was stronger than the other day. Olive and Bill must have replaced it so that the place would feel welcoming for Sally when she returned.

"Okay. So, we're looking for a USB or files with customer information. Either it's in plain sight or hidden, but if the police missed it, my tip is the latter."

"Agree." Donna peered into the bedroom. "I'll take in here."

"Sure. I'll do the bathroom. Use the light on your phone, though, not the torch."

They both put on their gloves and parted ways.

The bathroom felt smaller in the dark. Audrey checked the drawers and pockets of the blue toilet bag. It was empty. Then behind hair products, deodorants, and the rest of the drawers. Nothing. On the corner of the bath was a container of soaps. Nothing there either. Nor in the small plant holder on the other corner.

"Come on, Sally. Where is it?"

Kneeling on the floor, she scanned under the drawers using the light from her phone. The ceiling fan? It looked built-in. An electrician was needed to remove the cover.

Confident it wasn't here, she headed back to Donna. "Any joy?"

Donna had her hand under the base of the mattress. "Not so far. I've checked the drawers, wardrobe, inside jackets and shoes, behind the print, and all the bedding. If it's here, I can't find it."

What was the easiest place to hide something, but the most difficult to check? "Let's try the kitchen," said Audrey.

Donna stood and brushed off the front of her pants.

The floorboards creaked as they made their way towards the rear of the house. It was a clear night, so the moonlight helped light up the otherwise dark room.

"I'll take the drawers and cupboards," said Donna.

That left Audrey with the pantry. She pulled out a chair and stepped on top to look inside. On the top shelf were one-kilogram bags of coffee beans. Sally liked her coffee and bought in bulk. Below that was an assortment of rice and pasta packets. The open ones had secure clips to prevent them from going stale. At home, half-open packets had an elastic band around them at best or were left open. The next shelf down housed a collection of sauces and spices. The bottom shelf contained tinned products — soups, tomatoes, and beans. The layout looked similar to her own, that of someone who cooked at home most nights, except here everything was in its right place, perfectly lined up, and Audrey would bet it was all in date. Not something her own pantry could claim.

She moved items on the top shelf, careful to move them back to their original position. Nothing there. Repeating the action on the second shelf gave the same result. She was about to climb down to search the bottom shelves when something caught her eye. In the back corner was an opened box of packet soup. But soups belonged on the shelf below. Leaning in, she removed the box. Inside was a silver sachet. One end was open. And inside was the USB. She smiled. "Found it."

Donna closed a cupboard above the sink. "You're kidding me."

Audrey held up the USB, victorious, suddenly realising she should have brought a laptop or something to copy it onto. Her heart sank. Now they would have to come back.

"Your place or mine?" Donna grinned.

Audrey checked the time. Mark and the kids would be at the movies, which meant they wouldn't be interrupted. "Mine's closer."

They returned the key and left.

Audrey hurried into the kitchen and plugged the USB into her laptop. Donna slid into a chair alongside her, grinning. If they could find a motive for Sally's disappearance, they might know where and even who to look at. A single file titled *File* appeared on the desktop.

"Here goes," said Audrey.

Donna clapped her hands excitedly.

Inside the file were more files with dull names. *File 1. File 2.*

Donna frowned. "She's not that imaginative with the file names."

Audrey clicked on *File 1*. A stream of files with customer names appeared. *Aaron's Liquor Store. Art's Crafty Place.* There were hundreds of customer files in alphabetical order.

Donna sat up, excited. "That's more like it."

Audrey clicked on *Aaron's Liquor Store*. Inside were PDFs of customer orders and a single Word document: Sally's notes on the customer. Days they were available. Their best contact details. Typical information that would go into a customer database.

"When Mark and I met her customer the other night, he said Lucas and Trish had a sales rep steal information before, which is why they didn't want to buy a database. Looks like she's created her own."

Audrey felt a pang of disappointment. But was this all there was?

"Mind if I look?" said Donna, itching to take the keyboard.

Audrey pushed the laptop towards her.

Donna clicked through the files at impressive speed. "Each one of these customer files has a Word document with Sally's notes and a summary of sales for this financial year."

Donna opened an Excel document showing Sally's total sales by month. She continued searching, then stopped. "Check this out."

Audrey leaned in. It was a company balance sheet. "Why does an employee have a copy of the balance sheet?"

"Good question." Donna lined up the balance sheet and Sally's sales figures alongside one another, scanning the information.

"Sally's sales alone were higher than the figure declared as income."

What did this mean? That the business was evading paying tax. The penalties were high. Donna brought up the browser and typed in *penalties for tax evasion in Australia*. Up to ten years imprisonment.

"Do you think they found out Sally has this information?"

And if they did, was this the motive for her disappearance?

"Maybe she confronted Trish and Lucas, and knowing the penalties, they freaked out and had something to do with her disappearance?"

It felt like a long shot but wasn't impossible.

Audrey thought back to their meeting with Lucas. "Lucas seemed pretty broken up about Sally's disappearance, unless it's guilt."

"So what do we do now?"

It was a good question. "We can't let the police know we found this, obviously."

The days of using a "tip from a source" and maintaining anonymity for that source were on shaky ground.

Audrey took another USB from her bag. "Can you copy it to this?"

Donna took the USB and began making a copy.

"We need to put this back."

Regardless of whether she could lead the police to it, all hell would break loose if Sally returned and it wasn't there. "And then somehow get the police to find it."

Donna looked at her. "How are we going to do that?"

"That's the bit I have to sleep on."

31

The USB was back in Sally's pantry and Donna now at home. Audrey drove along the highway towards home, passing only the occasional car. Tomorrow it would be five days since Sally was reported missing. She looked out over the black inkiness of Port Phillip Bay to her left. *Where are you, Sally?*

Over fifty thousand people were reported missing in Australia every year. Every day that passed made the chances of finding her less likely. The police would soon move on to other cases unless new information came to hand and Sally's case changed from missing persons to suspected murder.

Did Audrey have that information?

She had to tell the police what she knew, whatever the fallout. Audrey dialled Cath's number, hoping she was on duty.

Cath answered. "Twice in one night. This better be good or quick or preferably both."

"Ten minutes, tops."

"You better hurry. I'm about done for the day."

Audrey drove down Chilton Hill towards Bennington Police Station, trying not to go over the new painfully slow speed limit.

Moments later, she removed her jacket and took a seat opposite

Cath, who placed a manila folder—presumably with information on Sally Child—in front of her. She looked tired. It was best to get to it.

"I mentioned I met some of Sally's customers at the brewery the other night. They said that Sally was the best salesperson by a country mile, but that things weren't all rosy."

Cath opened the file and checked the notes but offered nothing, so Audrey continued.

"Sally was unhappy about stock issues and the lack of a customer database, but the owners were worried about information being stolen, so they weren't keen on installing one."

Cath's face remained expressionless, but she made a tiny note. "Nothing out of the ordinary there. Plenty of people are unhappy with their employers for not giving them what they wanted."

It was a fair point.

"But tonight at the brewery, the same customer said she must have detailed notes somewhere because she was so good at remembering things. It sounded like Sally had created her own offline customer database."

Cath was listening. "Which is why you asked me if there was anything on her computer."

"Correct. What if Sally, who likes to be organised, sets up her own records on the business, and her bosses find out? They're worried about employees stealing information, but now they're terrified she might leave and take valuable information to a competitor."

Cath frowned. "Because Sally kept files on her customers, you think this is why she went missing?"

Hearing it out loud, it sounded far-fetched. Audrey was tired and briefly felt her resolve slipping.

"It would have to be good information," said Cath.

It was. Now Audrey had to lead Cath and her team to it.

"I can see how this sounds, but what if that information was damning or sensitive? What if it was more than customer information? It would speak to motive."

Motive changed things. It could move the status of the case from missing persons to suspected murder. It meant a whole different level of resources assigned to the case. Perhaps even prevent Sally from being relegated to the "long-term missing," a kind of purgatory hell for family and friends who never got answers.

"Which, correct me if I'm wrong, you don't have."

Cath's mouth tightened. "No, we don't. But we searched the house."

Audrey needed them to do it again.

With luck, Cath would see the potential in the threads Audrey was about to present.

"So, if the information is not on her computer, it's probably on a USB, which can be very difficult to find."

Like in an empty soup packet in the back of the pantry.

"Maybe it was missed in the initial search?"

A flash of suspicion crossed Cath's face. "Anything you're not telling me?"

Audrey shook her head.

Cath looked at her for so long, she was starting to feel uncomfortable, but then finally spoke.

"Let's just say I send some of my guys around to do another search, and they find this company information, and we look into those files and it's not good for the business. Any thoughts on what happens after that?"

It was time to let Cath know someone had been at the house, possibly looking for this information without putting herself in it. The idea had come to her on the way here.

"I visited Sally's house with Bill and Olive to have a look around. This was before I knew Sally kept company information on file, and no, I don't know where it is. As you know, they have a key safe. While Bill was removing the key, Olive stood next to me, muttering the code. So, I'm wondering how many other people know the code?"

She hoped Cath was reading between the lines and continued.

"Maybe someone went to Sally's to look for the information. Maybe they thought she was on a date, but she came home early and found them?"

Cath sat back, processing this information. "That's a lot of maybes."

"I know, but I thought it was worth letting you know."

Cath looked down. "You want our team to take another look inside Sally's to see if we can find this information? That it?"

"That's it."

With any other detective, Audrey would wonder if this information would be followed up on or remain a note in a file. The beauty of knowing someone for so long meant you could recognise a glint in their eyes. Cath was a fellow bloodhound. No stone unturned. If the police found the USB and what was on it, the investigation would spin in a whole other direction.

Audrey now had to hope they found it.

32

Asleep, awake. Time blurred. Her lungs felt tight, and opening her eyes was an effort. It was only a matter of time. No one was coming for her. *Was it time to concede defeat?*

Her will was in order. Her parents would get the house, which would pass to Rick one day. Hopefully, by then he would have his act together financially. Not that it mattered now. If he was really stuck, he could live in it, but they should make him pay rent, or he'd never learn. She pictured her parents and Di and Rick and Craig arriving to clear everything out. There would be tears and emotion, but eventually they would get to work.

Di would take her clothes and personal items, except for the woollen aqua and orange scarf, which she had promised to Katrina in accounts. Di was thorough and would take too long, which would frustrate her father, so eventually she would load everything into her car to go through it properly at home.

Her parents would take her photos and books, but the rest would go to charity. Her heart sank. All those years of carefully looking after her possessions, and now a stranger got to rummage through it and toss the bits that wouldn't sell.

Her mum would empty the kitchen. The fresh food would go into the cooler box Rick had bought when he went to Eden to fish. The tins and dry food would be loaded into cartons. *The soup packet.* It was the safest place she could think of. No one would find the USB there.

Nothing had prepared her for what she stumbled upon. There was no one around the day she walked into Lucas's office. The laptop was sitting there, open, facing away from her. She'd suspected something was going on. The refusal to install systems to do her job properly made no sense. Which was why when she saw the finances directory open, she sent herself a copy and deleted the email. If the business was in financial trouble, she had to know.

Gavin. She remembered now. Leaving the office, she'd run into him in the hallway. He looked surprised to see her.

"Everything okay?"

"Yes. I'm running late," she said, rushing past him.

It wasn't until she made it home that night that the enormity of what she'd done hit her. She had to know what type of people she was working for. She was a good person and would only work for good people. If the business was in trouble, maybe she could help. It didn't take long to find out. She was so disappointed.

Would her mother find the USB or throw it out as rubbish? If she was having a good day, she would hand it to her father. He wouldn't know what it was, but would ask his sister, who would realise the numbers didn't match. They would go to the police. *Was this why his daughter was missing?* It would take months to investigate, but eventually, they would be caught.

But what if her mum threw out the empty packet? Her father liked a good cull. What if she wanted to please him? Show him that despite being a hoarder, she could throw things out? It was the part of her mother's illness that bothered her most.

The more she deteriorated, the greater the need to please her father. Like he was her lifeline, and she had to keep him on the side for fear he'd abandon her, or worse, pull the plug. But there was nothing to fear. Her father adored her mother.

Sally was listed as a medical treatment decision-maker alongside her father. It was a point of contention with Rick, but they all knew he'd be a blithering mess and was unable to bring any logic to the situation when the time came.

A disturbing thought came to her. Had someone found out she

had copied the file? She had deleted the email, but there was always a trace. But to look, someone had to suspect something. The laptop was open when she arrived and when she left.

Did Gavin suspect she found something she shouldn't have? Surely, he would come and speak with her about it. They were friends. He wanted it to be more, but they had moved past that. He would never go behind her back. *Would he?*

He had been distant of late and was always trying to please Trish and Lucas, hoping they might one day give him a promotion or pay rise. *Had he told them she was in the office, snooping around?*

If Lucas checked the timestamp, *did he know she had information that could send them to prison?* Her mind swirled with possibilities. And if that was the case, *how far would they go to get it back and silence her?*

Please, Mum, don't throw the soup packet away.

33

Thursday

Audrey watched Josh climb out of the car. "Have a good day. Love you."

A mumbled "love you" came back as the door closed behind him.

Unlike Beth, who sprang out the door each day for school with enthusiasm, Josh's body language, sagging shoulders, and lumbering walk screamed he would rather be anywhere else. Only a few more years to go, my darling boy.

As she waited for the school queue to move, her phone rang. Cath.

Had they found the USB already?

Excited, she answered. "Cath."

Cath lowered her voice. "We've found Sally's date. I'm at his home now. We're leaving soon to take him back to the station, so you'll need to hurry."

The interview with Olive and Bill had worked. "That's fantastic news."

So why didn't Cath sound happy?

Cath continued. "Cam Andrews has turned up, so I thought it was only fair you knew as well. Address is 24 Mason Drive."

Audrey knew the street. It was only five minutes away.

Cath would never divulge her initial thoughts on the man, so there was no point in asking. "Thanks for the heads-up. On my way."

Audrey sent a quick text to Donna. The paper's photographer would never get there in time, so her phone camera would have to do. She plugged the address into her GPS and after what felt like an eternity finally left the school queue. Why didn't Cath sound excited? And how did Cam Andrews find out so quickly? Did a contact at Bennington police or one of his loyal supporters tip him off? Regardless, she was grateful to Cath, who she hoped would never move on.

Sally's date lived in a smart, rendered home in Bennington South. A police car was parked in the driveway. Cam Andrews and his cameraman had finished setting up in the driveway and were checking they had the right view before he began broadcasting. Audrey hurried over. Cam acknowledged her and began his broadcast.

"I'm at the home of Leon Reeves, the man police have been wanting to speak with about local woman Sally Child's disappearance. Leon was the last person to see Sally alive after he says he escorted Sally to her car."

Cam checked his notes. "He states he then drove straight to a holiday rental in Gippsland to work for a few days. He claims the property didn't have signal, and so he only became aware Sally was missing when he returned home last night and subsequently made contact with the police. He denies having any involvement in Sally Child's disappearance."

Audrey detected the note of disbelief in Cam's voice and, for once, was inclined to agree. There were plenty of mobile and internet black spots in the area, but was it really possible he hadn't known Sally was missing for the past five days? But would a guilty person contact the police? Unless he thought someone would eventually identify him, so it was better to get in early.

The front door opened and Cath stepped onto the porch. Her jaw was clenched and her expression grim. It was impossible to get a read on her.

Cam stepped back so his cameraman could capture the footage. A slim, fit-looking man, medium build, wearing a Lacoste baseball cap and exercise pants, was being escorted by two police officers. So this was him. Audrey took photos with her camera.

It was hard to get a read on him without seeing his face. Cath climbed into the driver's seat. An officer escorted Leon into the back seat and climbed in next to him, quickly closing the door. The other officer climbed in the other side. Cam directed his cameraman to get footage of Leon as it backed out. All energy left the site as they drove away.

Cam gestured for his cameraman that he was ready. "The police will now interview Leon Reeves and determine whether charges need to be laid."

A woman in her fifties wearing black fitness wear and red lipstick approached Cam as he put his microphone away. "How long will it take before the police know if he's our guy, Cam?"

One of his trusty supporters?

Cam took this one. "It should be pretty easy to check out his alibi. They'll look at the time he says he left Sally to checking in to the rental. His employer can validate whether he took a few days off work."

A measured response for him.

"But who goes to a rental without signal to work? No one works offline these days."

There it was. The inflammatory remark he was known for.

"Right, Audrey?"

Cam's propensity to go for the story over facts annoyed her. No matter how much she hoped Leon Reeves would lead them to Sally, he deserved the presumption of innocence until proven otherwise.

"If his alibi checks out and the police think he's innocent, it might not take long at all to verify. However, if they think he's guilty, it will probably take time to build a case."

She hoped having Leon in custody didn't delay the search of Sally's house and finding the USB. The woman frowned. Audrey's response wasn't as interesting as Cam's.

Cam checked his watch. "We've got to keep moving. Off to a warehouse break-in over in Dandenong. Crime never stops. See you soon, Audrey."

Audrey gave a polite wave as Cam and his trusty sidekick headed off.

The woman was still there. "I bet her poor parents are happy they found him."

She walked away, already convinced Leon Reeves was guilty.

Sally's parents. How would Olive and Bill be taking this? The man who had last seen their daughter was now in police custody. They must be pleased there had finally been progress. Audrey was keen to find out.

34

Audrey didn't bother going via reception and walked straight towards Olive and Bill's unit. An elderly couple out for a walk smiled as she passed. A busy care worker in uniform was too engrossed in a phone call even to care who she was.

A moment later, she arrived at Bill and Olive's and knocked. Bill opened the door. She didn't know what to expect. Perhaps that he would be bright and alert about the news, but that wasn't the case. His eyes were puffy and his face pale. He looked frailer than ever.

Audrey was suddenly full of regret at the invasion of privacy. "Sorry, Bill. I should have called."

Olive appeared next to him in her dressing gown. Her hair was damp at the edges, like she was just out of the shower.

"Hello, dear." She didn't recognise Audrey.

Or was Olive's deterioration the reason for Bill's hangdog appearance?

An elderly couple stopped outside the property.

The woman spoke. "We're praying this is good news for you, Bill."

"That we are," said her husband in a Scottish accent.

Bill nodded to acknowledge the comment and gestured for Audrey to come inside before closing the door. "I take it you've heard the news?"

"Yes. I've come from his home."

"Right. Right." Bill gestured for her to sit down. He looked distracted, like he was weighing something up. "If I tell you something, can it stay in confidence?"

"Yes, of course," said Audrey.

"Apart from my sister, no one outside this room and the police know what I am about to tell you, but I'm keen to get your thoughts. See if they align with mine."

Audrey's pulse raced. She didn't know where this was going, but she sensed it was big.

Bill sat forward. "The police are looking at the freeway footage to validate the timing of his drive and check that he could have left Sally when he said. But his work have confirmed he was taking time off to work on a project, and there's proof he booked a holiday rental. A friend made a call, and he's being cooperative. Initial thoughts are that he's telling the truth."

Coming forward would have helped this perception as well.

Audrey wondered who Bill's friend was and if the call was to Cath but refrained from asking. "Was he able to confirm why he paid cash?"

Bill cleared his throat. "He was given cash by his mother for his birthday."

What is he, twelve?

Bill continued. "If his alibi turns out to be correct, what do you think it means?"

There was only one possible explanation. "That someone else was involved?"

Bill took a deep breath. "That's what I've been thinking."

There was little comfort in being on the same page. So much had been riding on finding Sally's date that it was devastating to think the perpetrator could still be out there. No wonder Bill looked like hell.

Olive sat up, lucid and on high alert. "Sally would have made sure her date walked her to her car. She would have got straight in and locked the door." There was not a hint of doubt. "But I don't understand how anyone could have hurt her if she was inside her car."

Bill wasn't convinced. "Things are different nowadays. Maybe he walked off without waiting for her to get inside."

Olive shook her head vehemently. "Sally would have insisted he wait. Do you remember how frightened she was after that woman in Brunswick was killed by that dreadful man? I know my daughter. She would have made him wait."

Bill wasn't convinced, but Audrey was inclined to agree with Olive.

Olive walked into the kitchen and took Sally's photo from the fridge.

Bill lowered his voice. "What if someone got to her before she got into her car?"

"Only a tiny percentage of attacks on women are by strangers. It's unlikely but still possible."

Bill went to help Olive, who was frozen, staring at the photo.

Audrey was grateful for a moment to think.

Had someone followed the couple and waited until Sally was alone? They would have to move fast before she got inside her car. But then how did they get her away from there? She didn't like it. And if Sally made it inside her car, it would be locked. She wouldn't open the window to a stranger. An idea circled. Unless it was someone she knew? In that case, she might even get out to speak with them. Would she get out and even go for a drink?

"Come on, love. Come and sit down." Bill ushered Olive back to the couch.

Audrey directed her question to both of them. "Did Sally ever mention any other male friends? Any other men she spent time with?"

Bill positioned Olive next to him and held her hand. "Apart from her brother, and Craig, and Gavin, no."

It wasn't a great question. Sally could have lots of friends her parents didn't know about. "Does anyone else know what you've told me?"

Bill shook his head. "I love my son, but he rushes in before he thinks. I'm meeting my sister, who's a lawyer, shortly, but for now we've been advised to keep things to trusted sources only."

Audrey was touched that she was considered in this camp.

Olive turned to Bill. "When's Sally coming with our coffee?"

Bill looked so tired. His daughter was missing, and his wife was losing her once competent mind. The man looked like he could do with a hug.

"How about I go to the cafe?"

Olive looked confused. "But what if Sally comes? Then we'll have two drinks."

"Sally might be late today," said Bill patiently. "Let's let Audrey get them."

Olive didn't respond, but Bill leaned over and picked up his wallet.

"Please let me get these," said Audrey. It was the least she could do.

35

She spotted the well-meaning couple who walked past Bill's earlier at a table by the window. The woman recognised her and whispered something to her husband. The appearance of Sally's date would be doing the rounds today.

A female barista wearing a trainee name tag took her order, then repeated it back to her. This could take a few minutes, so to fill in time, she read a community noticeboard with a range of tours and activities on offer. A person could be busy 24/7 in this place if they wanted to be.

The couple had been joined by two women. Well-meaning woman was holding court and the new arrivals listening intently to what she had to say. Were they talking about the news of Sally's date? Sally came to the cafe every day to get coffee for her parents. Perhaps the couple did too and knew something? The trainee had only just poured cold milk into a jug, so Audrey walked over.

"Excuse me. My name is Audrey, and I'm a friend of Olive and Bill's, but I also work at the *Gazette*. I wanted to ask whether any of you met their daughter, Sally."

Well-meaning woman responded. "Yes. She was a lovely girl. We used to see her on our walk down to the cafe each morning, didn't we, Isaac?"

"Is a lovely wee girl," said her husband, Isaac, correcting her. "Mary and I are both praying for her safe return."

Audrey had spent time in Scotland and tipped he was from Glasgow.

One of the other women, who had thick blonde hair like an elderly Marilyn Monroe, asked, "I haven't met her, but is it true she bought her parents a coffee every day so she could see them?"

Audrey answered, "Yes, she did."

Marilyn rolled her eyes. "I can't even get my son to call me back." She didn't look happy about it either.

"He's very busy with his work," said a birdlike woman.

Marilyn wasn't buying it and dismissed her excuses with a wave. "Rubbish. He's never forgiven me for telling him what I thought of that gold-digger he's shacked up with. I'm looking forward to the day when I can say I told you so. Hope I'm not dead before then."

Realising there were more important things right now than her daughter's choice of a partner, she added, "I hope she turns up. At least I know where my son is, thanks to his social media account. Not knowing…"

A solemn mood came over the table, but Audrey was keen to know if they knew Sally. "Have either of you met Sally?"

Birdlike woman and Marilyn shook their heads.

Audrey directed her next question to Isaac and Mary. "How did Sally appear to you? Did you ever see her upset about anything?"

The couple looked at one another, then Isaac spoke. "Quite the opposite. She was a happy lass. Always smiled and said good morning. You don't always get that these days with everyone on their mobiles."

Isaac put his palm towards his face to further illustrate the point.

"Did you ever see Sally with anyone other than her parents?" Anyone like Gavin. "I believe she used to come here with a friend sometimes."

Isaac had nothing to offer, but Mary did. "I saw her with a young man a couple of times. We live a few doors up from Olive and Bill's."

"His name is Gavin. About my height, brown hair."

Mary nodded. "That's him. They were always laughing and joking around. I think Olive was hoping they might start dating, but they were just pals. You can tell when someone likes someone that way. Can't you, Isaac?"

Isaac gave an embarrassed smile. A story for another time.

"Coffee for Audrey," the barista called.

She gestured that she was coming.

"I'm trying to find out as much about Sally's movements as possible. Sometimes even the smallest piece of information can help." Audrey handed her card to Mary. "If you think of anything else, please let me know."

Audrey left the foursome and collected her drinks.

Olive opened the door wearing a pretty cornflower-blue shift dress and ushered Audrey into the living room. "That's very kind of you to do that."

Audrey checked the lids and handed Olive her latte.

Olive removed the lid, smiling excitedly. "This is my favourite part."

Audrey placed Bill's coffee on the coffee table. "Where's Bill?"

"He's speaking with his sister. This is their day to have lunch, and they're working out where to go."

Audrey suspected Bill was discussing more than a lunch venue with his sister, the lawyer, following the events of the morning.

How did Olive fill in her time when Bill was gone? And if she was having a bad day, surely she couldn't be left alone. "What do you like to do when Bill is away?"

Olive sipped her coffee like it was the most delicious thing in the world. Audrey was pleased to bring the woman something that made her happy.

"I go to the cinema to watch a movie every week when they're at lunch. I'm going there soon."

Was this Bill's only respite for the week?

Audrey sipped her coffee. "Do many people watch the movies?"

Olive smiled. "Oh, yes. Sometimes the staff come and sit with us as well."

Audrey pictured overworked nursing staff taking a quick break to rest their feet.

"Alan sits with me while I watch the movie," said Olive.

An idea moved around Audrey's head, but it was just out of reach. "Is he one of the nursing staff?"

Olive shook her head. "No, no. He's one of the managers. We both like the classics."

Was it unusual for a manager to join a resident at the cinema?

"Does he sit with you every week or just sometimes?"

Bill was at the back door, finishing up his call.

Olive lowered her voice. "Every week, but don't tell Bill."

Audrey stifled a grin. Did Olive think Bill would get jealous?

"Alan told me not to tell anyone we sit together."

Why would he do that? Was it a breach of company policy, or was there some other reason? "What else do you and Alan talk about?"

Olive looked towards Bill and the back door. "Lots of things, really. But we sit up the back so we don't disturb anyone else."

Something felt wrong. She didn't know if it was the secretive nature of their catch-ups or that she felt protective of Olive, but she was keen to get a look at Olive's friend, Alan. There was only one way, and to do that she had to leave now.

36

The cinema was in a modern detached building five hundred metres from Olive and Bill's. A solid woman with a jolly, inquisitive face stood at the entrance of the theatre, welcoming residents to *The Philadelphia Story*. Audrey loved that movie and under different circumstances would happily have joined Olive.

A reception desk was on one side and at the far end were a long bench and a solitary plant. There was nowhere to hide, and anyone, including Olive, walking into the area would see her straight away.

The jolly woman looked over. "Can I help you?"

Audrey noticed the tiny crease in her forehead and had a feeling there would be more questions if she didn't go into the theatre or leave.

She remembered seeing a building with *wellness* in the title on the map. "Hi, I'm looking for the Wellness Centre."

The forehead crease disappeared. "Close, but it's farther up on the right. It's the new building with the timber slats out the front that tries to look like a day spa," but didn't quite succeed, judging by her brief eye roll.

"Thanks for your help."

Audrey stepped outside. Now what?

Opposite was an area of cleared land with patchy lawn and shrubs planted on the perimeter. The area was open, but there was no seating. On the far perimeter was a large oak tree with a thick trunk. She wouldn't be able to hear their conversation but could see them together. It wasn't ideal but would have to do.

Audrey made her way to the tree and pretended to check her phone while keeping one eye on the entrance. Fortunately, mobile phones provided an excuse to look busy.

Ten minutes later, Bill and Olive walked towards the theatre, arms linked. Olive was wearing gold slide sandals and a matching handbag. Her mind might be going, but she hadn't lost her sense of style.

Bill gently handed Olive into the care of the jolly woman, then hurried back in the direction he had come from for some well-deserved time off. Audrey's phone buzzed.

"Where are you?" Donna had news.

"I'm in the village with Olive and Bill. What's up?"

"Eve spoke to the police. Leon Reeves's story checks out. He saw Sally climb into her car and then walked back to his car parked on the Esplanade. He chatted to one of the chefs outside Kirks on the Esplanade who remembered seeing him."

"Right," said Audrey.

"Why do I get the feeling you know this?"

"Bill has a source in the police who confirmed as much," said Audrey.

Donna groaned. "Does that mean that it could be any weirdo?"

"Or someone she knows," said Audrey. "What if Sally was in her car, and someone she knew came to the window?"

A group of men wearing pants and business shirts walked towards the centre. They weren't dressed like staff or residents. Was Alan among them?

"Sorry, but I have to go. I'll be back soon."

Audrey moved behind the tree. The oldest of the group, a man in his fifties, pointed to the theatre building, and the group slowed. One of the younger men opened up a large sheet of paper—perhaps plans —for the others to look at. Were they architects or building consultants? Was Alan among them? They all leaned in to check the plans versus the building in front of them. After a brief consultation, the man rolled up the paper, and the entire group continued along the path towards the wellness centre.

Five minutes later, it was starting to look like Alan wasn't going to show. She didn't know how long the elderly woman on her balcony in the units behind had been watching her. Audrey smiled, but the woman didn't return the gesture. Security would be called if she didn't move soon. She was about to walk back across the lawn when a handsome man in a suit that looked executive or legal headed towards the theatre. A female nurse passed him and beamed. There was a confidence in his walk—not quite a strut—but this was a man used to female attention. He walked up the steps of the theatre and disappeared inside.

Was this Alan?

Audrey hurried across the lawn and into the foyer. Jolly woman had left. Good. She opened the theatre door a sliver so as not to let any light in. The theatre sat around a hundred and was half full. Olive liked to sit up at the back. Craning her neck, at first Audrey couldn't see her. But then she spotted her in the corner with the handsome man, whispering like the best of friends. Olive was pointing at the screen. The man was smiling. Olive didn't appear to be in any harm, and there were other patrons in the cinema. There was no way of listening in, so she closed the door. But as innocent as their catch-up looked, something niggled.

At reception, a sour-faced man in his late twenties looked up from a computer. "How can I help you?"

"I'm running late for a meeting with Alan. Don't suppose you've seen him?" She tried to sound light and breezy but wasn't quite pulling it off.

"Do you mean Alan Jenkins or Alan Taylor?" said the man with a stony face.

Audrey took out her phone. "Sorry, I've forgotten his surname."

The man glanced at something on his computer. "What's it got to do with?"

"Sorry. I've had an urgent email." She ignored the tiny frown on the man's face and quickly opened LinkedIn on her phone, hoping at least one of the Alans would be there, along with a photo. She typed *Alan Jenkins*. No photo. Ten connections. Registered Nurse.

It had to be the other Alan.

"Alan Taylor."

The man brightened. Was this the effect this guy had on everyone around him? "He just left. Do you want me to page him for you?"

Did she detect an eagerness in there as well?

"You know what? I've got his number. Why don't I call him? Sorry, don't know why I didn't think of that." Neither did the man, going by his pinched expression. "Thanks for your help."

Outside, she dialled Donna. "I want you to find everything you can on Alan Taylor who works at the Eliza James facility, either as an employee or as a consultant. I'm on my way back now."

37

Audrey arrived back in the office to find Donna at reception, Stan tapping at his computer, and no sign of Eve. Perfect. "How did you go?"

Donna was at her computer with several pages open on her screen. "He didn't make it easy. No Facebook or Instagram, at least not under his name, but he has a website page. He's a consultant specialising in technology solutions for the Australian aged care sector. By the looks of his clients, he started off in Queensland and then moved to Melbourne a couple of years ago. Eliza James is his biggest client, but he also works with two other smaller homes in the eastern suburbs."

"Is there a photo of him? He doesn't have one on LinkedIn."

"Not on his website, but I found one on an aged care conference page."

Donna moved so Audrey could see her screen. The photo was grainy, but there was no mistaking it was the same man. "That's him."

Stan leaned back and spun his chair towards them. "Why are you looking into this guy?"

She was keen to get Stan's take on things. "It feels odd that a consultant would befriend a resident with dementia a couple of months before her daughter goes missing."

Stan wasn't convinced. "You think he has something to do with Sally's disappearance." He sighed. "Bit of a leap?"

Stan had a point, but something about Olive and Alan's friendship bothered Audrey. "It might be nothing, or it could be something. Don't suppose you've got a few minutes while we go over what we know."

Stan stood and stretched. "Shoot!"

"I need a white board," said Donna, frustrated. "I put in a request a month ago."

"Good luck with that. I've been asking for a standing desk for about a year. Will be a damn sight cheaper than putting in an injury claim."

Was he serious? It was hard to tell.

Audrey cleared her throat. "Okay. Sally and her date went for a walk along the Esplanade. Leon walked Sally back to her car and then walked back to his car on the Esplanade after speaking with the chef. Someone could have approached Sally, but she wouldn't have opened the door unless it was someone she knew."

Or someone she had been keen on.

"Di mentioned that Sally had been keen on someone at the gym. She couldn't remember his name but thought it started with an A, like Olive's friend."

Stan stopped stretching. "I'm going to be Negative Nelly here, but do you know how many thousands of men's names start with A? Jan made me consider about every one of them. But I agree, it is odd he's hanging out with a resident with dementia."

Did Sally know where he worked and told Di? "Hang on." Audrey dialled Di's number. "Di. It's Audrey again. Sally's friend from the gym, the one she was keen on. Did she ever mention where he worked?"

Audrey listened. It was a long shot, but worth checking. "No. Okay. Thanks." Audrey hung up. "She doesn't know."

Donna sat forward. "Let's say Mr A, whoever he is, approaches Sally, and she winds down the window or even gets out of the car. We still don't know why he would want to hurt her."

Stan stood with hands on hips. "How about this? He's out, maybe looking for someone to go home with and spots Sally. He knows she's keen on him and tries it on."

"Even though he was the one who rejected her?" Audrey asked.

"Some guys will take whatever is on offer if you get my drift. She's over the moon because she was keen on him, and now voilà, here he is. They go off together somewhere private. She's hoping this will be a chance to get to know each other. He's got something else in mind. Things get a bit rough. She tries to leave, but he won't have a bar of it. Maybe even threatens to press charges. And, and if it is this Alan, it would be the end of his career. No aged care facility is going to let anyone on site with a record, especially when it comes out that he's been hanging out in the cinema with a resident with dementia."

Donna looked at Stan, impressed. "Good work, old man."

Stan gave a mock bow. He was enjoying this. Maybe Donna was right, and he wasn't ready for retirement after all.

Audrey agreed. "Okay, let's park that for a second. Then we've got what's happening at work. Sally took copies of sensitive information that could put her owners in jail for tax evasion. Then someone with the key safe code snuck into her house looking for something that may or may not have been the USB, but we think it's likely it was. We also know they left driving a VW Beetle."

Stan scoffed. "Chick's car."

Donna shook her head. "Not anymore. The latest ones are sportier with a track-inspired look and more horsepower."

Stan looked at Audrey. "You been watching *My Cousin Vinnie*?"

Donna looked confused. "What?"

Stan gave her a dismissive wave. "It's a movie. Before your time."

Donna looked miffed that she didn't get the reference.

"It's not Gavin's. He drives a Falcon sedan," said Audrey. "That doesn't mean he doesn't have access to one, but for now let's go with it being someone else."

"But whose is anyone's guess." Donna looked frustrated. "Most guys post their cars, and there's nothing on Rick or Craig's socials."

Were they looking for a relationship between Sally's work and Alan when they were separate, or were they related and not seeing the link?

Stan read her mind. "It could be purely opportunistic that

someone broke into her house once they figured she wasn't coming back."

"Maybe, or there's a link somewhere we're not seeing. Does Gavin know Alan? Or maybe Alan knows Trish and Lucas? Maybe Alan's a member of their VIP club, and he met them there?"

"How the hell are you going to find that out?" said Stan.

Audrey didn't know, but finding out where he lived felt like a starting point. "Don't suppose you've got a home address for Alan Taylor."

Donna shook her head. "Unfortunately, no."

"He goes to the gym the same nights as Sally, so he should be there tonight. We know what he looks like, so we could wait and follow him."

"And then do what?" Stan said, concerned.

Audrey wasn't sure. A lot of the time she worked on instinct, and right now it felt like the best option. "Not sure, but we'll work it out from there."

The phone rang, and Donna took the call. Stan walked over and placed both arms on her desk. Lowering his voice, he said, "Is everything okay?"

"Yes. Why are you asking me that?"

Unperturbed, Stan continued, "Sneaking around people's sheds late at night, and now following a guy who may or may not be dangerous. I mean, I know you like to go over and above, and it's not the first time you've followed someone, but I'm checking."

Audrey took it in the intended spirit. "I'm fine."

Stan's arms stayed on the desk. He wasn't done. "It's difficult for spouses to understand what it's like once you've got the sniff. Jan used to break my balls for working so long on certain stories. Those days are gone, but I remember what it felt like. In fact, going 'undercover' with Gavin the other night gave me a reminder. But if this guy is dangerous, you need to be careful." Stan removed his arms. "I'm here if you ever need to chat. Journo to journo."

"Thanks."

Grateful for the care, she was relieved when he returned to his seat. What was happening? There seemed to be some kind of subterranean tectonic shift taking place inside of her. Like certain parts of herself were shaking loose, bits of her old self falling away, leaving behind a sense of anticipation and unease like nothing she had experienced before. She didn't know what it all meant, but it felt like her life was subtly shifting direction, even if there was no clear destination in mind.

38

Audrey and Donna waited in the car outside Next Level Fitness. The entrance was one hundred metres away, but they had a clear line of sight as members came and went. It had been forty minutes since Alan Taylor entered, and Audrey was hoping he wasn't planning on a long session.

Sally's disappearance couldn't have been worse timing on the home front. Mark wasn't happy she was out for work again. A word to Josh to enlist his father to help with his biology assignment took the heat out of things, but that wouldn't take all night. Josh didn't have his sister's stamina for long, gruelling study sessions.

For the next twenty minutes, they watched members either beeline for their cars or stay on the steps, talking, passing the time by trying to work out who was keen on who. Which ones couldn't wait to escape. The introverts and the extroverts.

Donna pointed. "That's Lucas."

"I didn't know he went here," said Audrey.

They were so engrossed in a heated discussion about what that meant they nearly missed Alan leaving behind them.

"That's him." Audrey spun in her seat to follow Alan as he walked towards a car farther along in the opposite aisle. Freshly showered, judging by his damp hair, he was wearing sweatpants and a white T-shirt and carrying a gym bag. He climbed into the driver's seat and closed the door.

Donna craned her neck to see. "It's a Mazda 6. Dark grey. Couldn't get a more difficult car to follow if we tried."

Audrey started the engine, ready to try anyway. "Let's try not to lose him then."

The task was simple: find out where the guy lived to see if that gave any further clues about him.

Donna put on her seat belt. "Okay. Here he comes."

Audrey let Alan drive past and saw he stopped at the lights. Moving out slowly, she kept her distance until the lights turned green. He had no choice but to turn left on the highway, which made this part easier, at least. Alan turned left, and Audrey followed.

"Don't get too close," said Donna, "but also don't lose him."

Audrey kept several hundred metres between the two cars. The traffic was busy enough to blend in.

Alan pulled into the right lane and stopped at an island intersection.

"He's turning," said Donna, whose voice had risen.

Audrey had no desire to tuck in behind him, but going ahead meant they would lose him. Fortunately, Alan crossed the highway and headed through the industrial part of Bennington towards the freeway.

"Wonder where he's going," said Donna.

"Hopefully not to the city."

Audrey didn't picture that call to Mark going well. At best she had an hour before he would call. The lights were green. Alan's car drove through, then turned left, passing the freeway entrance. "Good. At least he's not heading to the city."

His car continued along the twin-lane highway for another kilometre until his right indicator turned on.

"He's heading to the Boroughs," said Donna. "What do you think? Going home or visiting someone?"

"Let's hope it's the former," said Audrey.

This was the second time she had followed someone into the Boroughs this week. First Gavin and now Alan. Hopefully, this time would be more productive.

Alan eventually pulled into the driveway of a tidy brick veneer home with a single carport and garage behind that.

Audrey parked on the opposite side of the street two houses down. He removed a laptop and gym bag from the back seat and headed inside.

"Gavin lives near here, right? They might have met at the local shops." But there was little conviction in Donna's voice. There was no need to point out it was a long shot.

It was one of the better streets in the area. One where people cared about their properties. One where they knew their neighbours? The house to the left of Alan's was dark. It was too early to sleep, so perhaps they were away. The one to the right had the front curtains open. A woman in her forties was exercising while a teenage girl sat on the couch on her phone. In the driveway was an old Ford Laser, a woman's car.

"I wonder whether he knows his neighbour."

"Maybe. What are you thinking?"

"I need something that looks like mail." Audrey checked the back seat and found an unopened magazine and in the console a utility bill. "I'll pretend I've got some mail for him and see what she says."

Donna grinned. "Nice one. I'm going to see if there's a window down the side of the garage and if there's a VW inside."

Was that safe? But if the car was there, it could move things forward in a big way. "Be careful."

They both climbed out. Audrey hurried to the house next door. Donna headed into Alan's driveway towards his garage.

Audrey knocked on the security door. A workout video stopped, and a clammy-faced woman, a little out of breath, appeared behind a security door. "Can I help you?"

Her voice was wary. It was night in the Boroughs, after all. Or was she expecting an unwelcome visitor?

Audrey smiled. "I'm looking for Alan Taylor. Does he live here?"

"Alan?" She looked interested, on high alert, and turned on the porch light. The door remained locked. "He lives next door," she said, gesturing to the house on her left.

"Sorry. I must have read the house numbers incorrectly. My

husband and I rent his old house, and we have mail for him. Sometimes you don't get around to changing everything."

Her eyes narrowed. "Isn't it easier just to post it?"

"Some of it looked pretty important. We've had a few things go missing in the post, and I wanted to make sure it got to him."

"I can give it to him if you like."

Was she looking for an excuse to catch up with her neighbour?

"That's okay. I'll make sure he gets it. By the way, this is a lovely street."

The woman finally opened the door. "I used to be over on Olivetti, so it's way nicer than there. You from around here?" She glanced over at Audrey's car.

"I grew up in Bennington and always had a lot of friends from around here." Some, like the Masters, she was happy to stay in touch with. Others, criminals like the Millers, she'd prefer to never see again. "We're hoping to buy in the area, but we want to rent and see if we like it."

The woman's face was full of longing. "I'd love to own this place. Casey goes to the high school around the corner. Same one I went to. And Alan, actually."

"Really?" Audrey tried not to sound too interested.

"He was a few years ahead of me, so we didn't know each other at school." Pity, by the look on her face. "We've both got the same tight-ass landlord, so sometimes we have a bitch about him, you know."

So, Alan was renting, and from the Boroughs.

"I thought Alan was from Queensland? Going by his mail."

"He was up there for a bit but came back a while ago. Not many people leave and come back here."

She was right. People stayed in the Boroughs, or they left. You didn't come back. Audrey couldn't think of a single reason why someone would return to the place.

A teenager girl's voice bellowed. "Mum. Show's about to start!"

It was time to go.

"I'll leave you to it," said Audrey, waiting until the woman closed the door before returning to the car.

She climbed into the driver's seat and closed the door. Donna was back in the passenger seat. "There's nothing except a couple of plastic tubs in the garage. How did you go?"

Audrey threw the fake mail onto the back seat. "He went to Boroughs High, moved to Queensland, and came back to the Boroughs. Why would someone come back to this place?"

"You came home," said Donna.

"Yes, because I couldn't get any other job. He could live anywhere else."

Was Audrey putting her own paradigm on things? Because she didn't want to return home didn't mean everyone felt that way. Had Alan gone out into the world, not found anywhere to settle, and returned to the place he had once called home? Maybe. But people also came to the Boroughs to hide. There was a code here: never snitch on your neighbours and look the other way. It was how the Millers got away with running their violent empire from their back porch without a single neighbour ever reporting anything unusual on their property. Did Alan have something to hide?

Donna asked, "What now?"

Audrey turned on the engine. "I need to speak to Olive about her friend Alan."

No time like the present. It would be quicker to go straight there, and Mark would be less annoyed if Donna was with her. "You good?"

Donna brightened. "Absolutely."

Audrey sent Mark a text then dialled Bill.

39

Bill was waiting for them at the door, also keen to understand why a consultant was accompanying his wife to the cinema. Audrey made a point of saying there was no proof Alan had anything to do with Sally's disappearance, but Bill was no fool and knew she suspected there was a link somewhere. Moments later, the foursome was seated in the living room with four glasses of water. Olive had on a floral dressing gown and silver slippers, ready for bed.

"Olive, I wanted to ask you about your friend Alan. The one who comes and sits with you at the cinema."

Olive's cheeks blushed. She glanced at Bill like she'd been caught cheating. Alan was a handsome, younger man, so perhaps there was some attraction on Olive's side.

"He's one of the staff. We both like the classics."

"We know that," said Bill. There was an edge to his voice that caused Olive to stiffen.

Audrey glanced at Bill, who sat back and let her take the lead. "What do you and Alan talk about? Apart from the movie you're watching."

Olive looked up like the answer was on the roof. "Goodness me. Many things. Mainly the actors in the film, which ones are still alive, that sort of thing. I like to watch the Academy Awards each year to see who's passed, but sometimes you miss someone."

"Did you and Alan ever talk about Sally?"

Olive's eyes flickered with concern. "Sally? I don't think so. Why?"

Her voice had risen. The mention of Sally's name had triggered something.

Audrey rephrased the question. "Did Sally ever come up in any of your conversations?"

"Not that I recall." Olive looked at Bill, her face full of concern. "Do you think he's involved in Sally going missing?"

Good. Olive had been able to join the threads, but Audrey had to tread carefully. She couldn't go around accusing the man without proof. "I'm not saying that, but do you recall ever speaking to him about Sally? Maybe talking about her work. Her friends."

The colour appeared on Olive's cheeks again. "I might have said how I wished Sally would meet someone. Maybe focus a little less on work and more on finding a husband."

Olive looked at Donna, then Audrey. "Every mother wants their daughter to have a child one day, and women only have a narrow window to make that happen. You have a daughter, don't you?"

Beth's sole focus was on academic excellence and then securing a high-paying job with prestige. Audrey wouldn't be surprised if she bypassed motherhood altogether.

"Yes, but she's only a teenager, so plenty of time for all that." Audrey tried another approach. "Did Alan ever say he knew Sally?"

Olive shook her head. "No. Did he know Sally?"

Audrey smiled to help her relax. "We think they might have been friends from the gym."

Olive's eyes darted around as what was left of her once sharp mind tried to work out what this could mean. "Why wouldn't he tell me he knew Sally? That doesn't make sense."

It did if you wanted to get information about someone without it looking suspicious.

Olive's breathing became fast and laboured. Her arms trembled slightly as she clenched the fabric of her dressing gown. She was getting uncomfortable, so Audrey changed tack. She didn't want the woman to shut down or to cause more distress than was necessary.

"Did you talk to Alan about any of Sally's friends, or did he ever ask about them?"

A sudden spark of recognition crossed Olive's face. Her posture changed and her shoulders stiffened.

Bill saw it too and sat forward, gently taking his wife's hand. "Anything, love. No matter how small."

The warm gesture calmed Olive, still wrangling the thought.

People with dementia often found it confusing and frustrating to recall the words or concepts they wanted to express. Memory lapses and difficulties connecting different ideas only made it more challenging to complete tasks or solve problems. On top of that were feelings of anxiety, frustration, and confusion. Audrey willed Olive to catch the thought.

"One day, he asked me about Gavin. Sally and Gavin had been over, and we walked with them back to reception. You remember, Bill?"

Bill nodded, although judging by the look on his face, he was also trying to work out why a consultant would be asking about Gavin.

Olive continued, "I remembered seeing Alan up the hallway. The next time I saw him, he waved and asked about Gavin."

"Why was Alan asking about Gavin? Did he know Gavin or recognise him from somewhere?" Audrey could hear the eagerness in her own voice.

"I don't think so. To be honest, I can't recall. I think he asked if that was my daughter, which seems odd now if you say they know each other. I didn't think anything of it."

Was Gavin the link between the brewery and Alan? Gavin didn't look like he went to the gym, but maybe they had met somewhere else? The earlier optimism vanished, and now a heaviness settled over the room.

Audrey had hoped Olive would divulge a snippet so everything would make sense. You needed a good dose of optimism in this profession, but too much wasn't good either. Bill sensed it too and headed into the kitchen for a glass of water.

As Audrey contemplated her next move, Olive spoke. "I did see Alan at Bunnings one day with Craig."

Audrey and Donna looked at one another. What the hell? Bill heard it too and hurried back next to Olive's side.

"You remember, Bill. You wanted a new light on your bed. I waited in the car because it started raining, and I'd had my hair done."

Bill looked at Audrey. "Yes. Yes. That was three weeks ago."

"Where did you see them, Olive?" Audrey asked.

Olive brightened. "They were standing at the sausage sizzle. Craig was eating a sausage when Alan came out. They only chatted for a minute, and then Alan left, but Craig didn't look happy when he left. I'd forgotten all about it until now."

Olive looked pleased with herself for remembering it. What was the connection between Craig and Alan?

"Does Craig go to the same gym as Sally?" Audrey asked.

Bill's face was grave. "I don't know, but his cousin Ash is the manager there."

Donna had been silent until now but gasped.

40

———

Audrey dialled Craig's number while Bill and the others watched on. It took several rings before he answered.

"Craig. Hi. It's Audrey Lord. From the *Gazette*."

In the background was the hum of conversation. Was he at a conference?

"Oh, hi. I'm in Sydney. Not much to report on Sal, though, I'm afraid."

"I'm actually here with Olive and Bill and my colleague Donna. If it's okay, I'd like to put you on speaker and ask you a couple of questions."

"Sure."

Audrey put the call on speaker as a voice came over the public address system, announcing the next session was starting in five minutes.

"Hi, everyone. Hang on. I'll step outside for a sec. Overdue for some fresh air."

The chatter stopped, replaced by light traffic. "Okay, shoot."

The guy travelled a lot.

Audrey continued. "Do you know someone called Alan Taylor from the gym?"

"Hi. Yeah, I know him." Craig's voice was frosty. "Why are you asking about him?"

Audrey had to tread carefully. "Are you two friends?"

"I wouldn't call us friends, but I know the guy. Bit standoffish. A few guys from the gym go out for a beer sometimes. We asked him a few times, but he always made some excuse, so we stopped asking. Why the interest?"

Craig sounded cautious but wasn't giving anything away.

Audrey tried to sound light. "Di said Sally was keen on someone at the gym, and we were wondering if that was him?"

Craig's voice lightened. "Sal speaks to everybody, but she never mentioned him to me."

Audrey sighed.

"But if she did, I'd be steering her clear of him."

The others moved in closer to the phone.

"Why is that?"

Sometimes the glacial pace of journalism killed her.

"Everyone knows everyone back home, right?" Craig said.

They didn't call it the insular peninsula for nothing.

"Few weeks ago, I see him coming out of a lady I know, Cara's place. Our kids play soccer, and I used to drop her kid off after training sometimes. I was about to wind down the window and say hi when Cara comes flying out the front door after him, yelling and screaming. Didn't know they knew each other, but it wasn't a good time to stop for a chat, you know. I was going to keep driving when all of a sudden, he walks back, grabs her by the throat, and hurls her against the side of the house. Cara breaks away and runs into the house. He runs back into the house, but she's locked him out."

Olive looked horrified.

"What happened then?"

Did Craig stop or keep going?

"He looked a bit crazy, you know, and I didn't feel like getting my head kicked in, so I pulled over and waited to make sure she was okay. I could hear him screaming at her on the porch. The whole street could have heard, but then he got in his car and sped off. I saw her at soccer and she seemed fine, so I didn't mention it. Thought she might be embarrassed, you know."

"Did you tell anyone else about this?" Audrey asked.

"I told Ash, but he thought I was exaggerating. I used to get into a few fights when I was younger, and he thinks I see trouble where there isn't. But I know what I saw."

Cath Maguire could find out if Alan had any violent priors.

"Olive said she saw you with Alan outside Bunnings recently."

"Yeah. I was going to say something about Cara, let him know I saw him, but I left it. Put me off my food seeing him."

Audrey was keen to speak with Cara. "I don't suppose we could have a chat with Cara? I need to ask her about Alan."

There was a long silence before Craig said, "Do you think he's got something to do with Sal?"

Audrey had no proof. "I don't know, but right now I'm keen to explore all avenues."

"I don't have her number, but I could probably find her address with the help of Google Maps. Give me a few minutes."

"Thanks."

Audrey hung up.

Bill was comforting a pale-looking Olive. "But what if he hurt Sally? And what if I told him something I wasn't meant to?"

The poor woman looked distraught.

Audrey turned to Donna. "I forgot to ask about the car."

"Call him back."

Audrey gestured for Donna to join her as she stepped outside to give Olive and Bill a moment alone and dialled Craig.

"I'm looking for her address now."

"I meant to ask; do you know anyone who drives a VW?"

"A VW. Sure. My folks. Dad's brother passed away and left it to him a couple of years ago. Why are you asking?"

"A VW was seen driving away from Sally's the other night after she went missing."

"You're kidding. Well, it wasn't my folks. They're in Darwin."

"Any chance someone else might have borrowed it?"

"Sure as hell hope not. And if they have, they didn't ask me."

"Is anyone staying at the property while they're away?"

"No. Mum hates the idea of other people being in her house, even though they could get a bomb for it as an Airbnb. I call past every weekend to make sure everything looks okay. Didn't get there last weekend because Sal went missing, but I'll be heading over when I get back."

That meant the property had been unattended for almost ten days. Craig was an open book and often posted his movements online.

Donna whispered. "We need to see if it's there."

Audrey agreed.

"Now you've got me worried someone's taken it. I might ask Rick to do a drive-by. Make sure it's there, although God knows when he can get there."

The front door opened, and Bill stepped outside. Audrey wanted to know if the car was there tonight. "We're happy to call past and check."

"I don't know." Craig sounded hesitant, which was understandable. They had only met twice.

She quickly brought Bill up to speed. "Craig's parents have a VW, but they're away, so we want to check it's still in the garage. There's a chance someone stole it, and that person was at Sally's."

This was a sufficient explanation for Bill. "I can go with Audrey if you like, Craig. I know where you live."

"That works. Keys are in the drainpipe next to the door, Bill."

"I'll let you know what we find," said Audrey.

41

Craig's parents lived in Pearcedale, a township and rural area on the northwestern corner of Western Port and ten minutes from Bennington. The relatively flat land with rich and sandy soil made it ideal for market gardening. Properties were a mix of smaller blocks and larger homes. Audrey slowed along a road with paddocks on either side, looking for a mailbox or entrance. The fading light made it harder to see.

Bill sat forward, trying to recognise the place. "I haven't been here for about twenty years, so things have changed a bit." He waved his finger like a wand. "This is it coming up. The one with the blue mailbox."

Audrey detected a hint of relief. She slowed and turned into the long dirt driveway that presumably led to a house not yet visible.

"This is so lovely here," said Olive from next to Bill.

On days like today, yes, but it wasn't so lovely in the rain. And in winter, it rained a lot.

Moments later, the dirt changed to gravel and then to a circular area with a fountain that looked like it had been out of circulation for a while. Behind it was a large, single-level brick home.

"That fountain wasn't working last time I was here."

Bill sounded unimpressed.

Audrey parked out the front of the house.

"Do I need to take my handbag?"

Audrey glanced at the couple in the rear-view mirror. Bill's days must be full of similar perfunctory instructions. "Not this time. It'll be safe in the car."

Bill helped Olive unbuckle her seat belt while Audrey and Donna climbed out. Donna gave Audrey a look. How cute are these two? Audrey wished they had met under different circumstances.

On both sides were green paddocks. She waited for Bill and Olive to climb out. "How much land do Craig's parents own?"

"About ten acres, but it feels like a lot more because they can't see the neighbours. No chance of ever being built out."

Bill looked longingly out over the wide-open space. Eliza James was the right place for Olive, but he'd sacrificed his large garden to ensure she had the right care. It couldn't have been easy.

"The garage is up here on the right, if I recall correctly."

A track to the side of the house led to a double garage, which looked new compared to the house.

"You two go. Olive and I will be there in a sec," said Donna.

Deciding his wife would be fine without him for a moment, Bill strode towards the garage at impressive speed.

Audrey followed, the gravel crunching underfoot, and once again she was glad she wore flat boots.

Bill stopped outside the garage. A section of downpipe ran down a corner of the side wall, as Craig had said. "I might let you get the keys, if that's okay."

"Sure." Audrey leaned on one knee and put her hand inside, hoping there were no spiders. She felt the key that was held in place by a small magnet and handed it to Bill. He opened the garage and feeling along the wall turned on a light.

The garage was a work of art. Along the left-hand side was a clean workbench, at the rear a spotless ride-on lawn mower, a leaf blower, and an assortment of tool cabinets on wheels tucked neatly alongside one another.

Bill wandered in first. "Bob keeps a nice, tidy garage." He looked impressed.

Audrey agreed, but her eyes were quickly drawn to the right-hand side and the empty space. "The car's gone."

This wasn't good.

Bill frowned. "Craig won't be happy."

A car cover had been thrown in one corner. Bill walked over and was about to pick it up, but they shouldn't touch anything in case it was later deemed a crime scene.

"Bill. It's probably best if we don't touch anything."

A grave look passed over his face, but he understood and made his way over to the expensive-looking ride-on mower.

The best thing they could do now was ring Craig and tell him his car was missing, report this to Cath, and leave. Audrey was about to suggest that when she spotted a gap at the end of the wall.

The makeshift wall ran three quarters of the length of the garage wall. She peered around it and stepped inside. On one side was a metal shelf with glass bottles on the top shelf and stainless-steel pots on the ones below. On the ground were plastic tubs. It looked like some sort of home-brewing operation set up behind the wall to protect the car. At the far end were four wine barrels stacked two across. A stamp on the front said Bennington Brewery. Audrey knocked on the two barrels closest to her. Both were empty. A large esky sat on the back of the last two barrels.

"Where have you gone?"

"In here, Bill," Audrey yelled.

Bill followed her inside. "What's this?"

"Looks like some sort of home-brew operation. The barrels are from Bennington Brewery."

Bill pointed to a photo of Craig and an elderly man, presumably his father, standing in front of the four barrels in a trailer.

"They did well to get those. Sally was always saying they kept running out of them."

"They did well getting hold of them then?"

Audrey tried to keep the suspicion out of her voice.

"Craig's been a customer of the brewery for years. He was the one who told Sally about the job. When they moved, he must have negoti-ated a few for himself."

That was one scenario.

Bill looked uncomfortable being in here. "We should let Craig know about the car. I'll call him if you like." He walked outside.

Audrey took another look around the garage. Her garage was tidy, but this was next-level. Returning to the home-brew room, she cast a final eye over its contents, looking for anything out of place. The cooler bin. It didn't belong here. She walked back into the garage. An esky similar in size was tucked in next to the work bench. Next to it was space for the second esky. So, why was the other esky in the home-brew room? Was there something inside?

Returning to the barrels and using the end of her sleeve so as not to leave fingerprints, she spun the esky sideways and lifted the handle. It was empty. Huh. She closed the lid and went to turn it back. Underneath was an empty space. A barrel was missing. Had whoever took the car also stolen a barrel?

"Hello." It was Donna.

But a barrel wouldn't fit into a VW. "In here."

Donna stepped behind the wall and joined Audrey. "Home brew or crystal meth?"

"The former, I think. The car's gone."

Donna spotted the photo of Craig and his father with the barrels. "So I heard."

Audrey spun the esky towards her. "Notice anything?"

Donna walked over and then back to the photo. "There's a barrel missing."

Audrey gave her a minute to see if she came up with the same thought.

"What if whoever took the car stole a barrel and... But hang on, a barrel won't fit into a VW."

Audrey's phone buzzed. She read the text. "Craig sent me the address of Cara, Alan's old girlfriend. Let's get Bill and Olive home and see what she has to say."

There were too many loose threads, but Audrey could feel them tightening. She only hoped they weren't going to be too late for Sally.

42

Audrey apologised to Cara's neighbour, a man in his sixties, and hurried next door with Donna. Craig had given them the wrong house, but it was an easy mistake to make. The properties looked almost identical. Audrey knocked on the modest brick home in Bennington, and a moment later a woman in her late thirties opened a security door in pants and a business shirt.

"Hi. Cara?"

"Yes."

"My name is Audrey Lord. I'm a journalist with the *Gazette*, and this is my colleague, Donna."

Donna smiled. "Hi."

Cara's face was understandably full of questions.

"I'm a friend of Craig's—one of the dads from your son's soccer team. I was wondering if we could ask you a few questions?"

There was no offer to come in, but she opened the security door. "What's this about? Has something happened to Craig?"

Cara looked worried.

"No. Craig's fine. We'd like to speak with you about Alan Taylor."

All joy left the woman's face. "I don't want to talk about him. Sorry, what's this got to do with Craig?"

"Craig was driving past recently and saw you arguing with Alan. He said things looked pretty heated."

Cara's cheeks flushed. "That's embarrassing, although I think the whole street heard."

"We believe Alan may know a woman who's recently gone missing."

The front door of the house they had been at earlier opened, and Cara's neighbour, an elderly man, walked out and opened the boot of his car. Did he need something, or was he trying to listen?

"It's important. She's been missing for five days."

Cara glanced at her neighbour, who didn't appear to be in any hurry, and opened the door. "You can't publish anything I tell you."

It wasn't a question.

"No. Not without your permission. We want to help find what happened to Sally Child."

Cara recognised the name. "I suppose you better come in."

They followed Cara down into a kitchen dining area. The room was sparsely furnished but neat and tidy. Photos of Cara and her two children, who looked about eight and six, were dotted around the room. The father didn't feature in any of them.

Audrey gestured to a picture of both children. "I've got a boy and girl too, but they're teenagers."

Cara gave a wary smile. "Brian's seven, and Lulu started school this year. They're at my mum's tonight. Would you like a drink?"

"We're fine." It was getting late, and Audrey was keen to get to it. "Could you tell me how you met Alan?"

Cara gestured for them to sit at the dining table. She sat opposite them with her hands clasped. "I met him through a party at the gym. My cousin goes there, and he asked me to come along."

Audrey sat forward. "Can you tell me about him?"

The flush receded from her face, but her hands remained clasped. "Great at first, but a few weeks later he started getting annoyed at me for nothing. It made me nervous, and I'd make even more mistakes. I'm not bragging, but I'm good at my job. But the minute I got around him, I became this pathetic creature."

Audrey spotted the laptop on the kitchen bench. "What do you do for a living?"

"I run my own travel business. I was with a franchise group, but I had to find my own clients anyway, so after a while I got sick of paying commission and went out on my own. I also look after private holiday properties for friends and friends of friends." Cara's face hardened. "I won't let anyone do that to me again."

Audrey's voice was gentle. "Do you mind telling us what happened the night Craig saw you arguing? We need to understand what this man is like."

The colour returned to Cara's cheeks. "I was having a shower and remembered I'd bought a new loofah, which was in my handbag. I can see into the kitchen from my room, and when I stepped out to grab it, I saw him on my laptop."

Audrey spun around. A bedroom had a line of sight to the kitchen.

"That's my private information. I should have yelled out, but instead I hurried out of the shower and banged around so at least he'd get off. He was going to stay for dinner, but suddenly he had to leave. I'd organised for the kids to go to Mum's and bought nice food that I couldn't really afford... I kind of lost it. I saw him walking out the gate and yelled that I saw him on my computer and asked what he was looking for."

Cara gulped. "Then he walked back and grabbed me by the throat and pushed me up against the house and said if I said anything, he'd kill me."

Cara's voice went quiet. "I'll never forget the look in his eyes. I believed him."

A respectful silence settled over the room.

"After he was gone, I checked and saw he'd opened a file with all my clients' private details. Key safe numbers. If word got out that my data had been stolen..."

Cara's business would be ruined.

"I probably should have gone to the police, but I was too scared for me, my kids, and so I did nothing. I couldn't ring my clients, so I waited for one of them to say something was stolen, but no one had. I'm hoping he's forgotten about me. You won't say anything, will you?"

Audrey declined to comment. She had no desire to ruin Cara's business, but her evidence might become crucial later on. "What do you think he was looking for?"

Cara looked genuinely perplexed. "I don't know. No one reported a robbery or any money going missing, and I talk to these people all the time. Maybe he was trying to work out how much money I make. I don't know. After that, I moved all my clients' confidential details to an online vault."

But Alan was after something.

Donna leaned in. "You said you also look after rental properties. Was he interested in those?"

Cara shrugged. "He'd opened a calendar showing which properties were rented, but once I saw he'd been in the client files, I figured that's what he was really after. Do you think he might be interested in one of their properties?"

Donna looked at Audrey. Maybe. "Do you mind if we have a look at the calendar?"

"I suppose it's okay. I'm not sure there's much to show you."

Cara brought her laptop over to the table, typed in her password, and brought up a spreadsheet. She turned the laptop to face them. The property name and address were down one side and booking dates were highlighted in the columns across.

Donna put her hands out. "Do you mind?"

Cara slid the laptop towards Donna, who hid the irrelevant columns so only the current week when Sally went missing was showing. There were two properties with vacancies, one in Dromana, the other in Red Hill. Both were thirty minutes south of Bennington.

Donna typed the address of the Dromana property into Google Maps. A single-storey modern home with a double carport at the front on a quarter-acre block.

Cara came and stood behind Donna. "It's a popular property. People like the fact they can drive straight into the carport to get into the house."

Cara gasped, joining the dots. "You think he might be using one of my properties to hide that woman?"

Yes, but they couldn't say that. "We don't know that, but right now we need to consider all options."

Audrey hoped that would suffice.

Donna moved arrows to see the properties on either side. They looked almost identical. "Are the neighbours' holiday rentals as well?"

Cara shook her head. "No. They weren't happy at first because they've both got young kids, but we've had a good run of tenants, so they're okay now."

Anyone coming in and out of the place like this would be visible. Donna had come to the same conclusion and was typing in the address for the Red Hill property. On the screen was an isolated pin. She zoomed in. It was at the end of a long track. Street view showed a gorgeous old weatherboard house but no garage.

Audrey pointed to a structure at the far end of the property that showed as a single square. "What's this building?"

Cara leaned in to look. "It's a storage shed. The owners use it, but it's not available to anyone renting the place."

Audrey looked at Donna, eyes blazing.

It was a long shot, but was this where Sally Child had been hidden?

"We need the key to see if she's inside," said Audrey.

Cara hesitated. They were journalists and not the police, so she could refuse. Was she going to ask to come with them? Audrey could see her weighing the options. Go with them, but risk being near Alan Taylor again, or wait until the police investigated. By then, it could be too late.

"I promise we won't touch anything. We'll bring the key straight back, but we have to know if Sally's in that house."

After what felt like an eternity, Cara left the room and returned with a locked box. She removed a set of keys.

"I need these back tonight."

Audrey took the keys. "I promise."

43

Tonight was the night. His body pulsed with excitement at the final task. Sally Child would be entombed in a place only he knew about for eternity. He wished his father was here. It would make him proud.

The VW was parked where he had left it last night near a popular wine bar in Safety Beach. The locals would think it belonged to a customer who had one too many and would only notice if it was still there in a few days. Once he dropped it back in the garage, he'd leg it across paddocks to the main road and flag an Uber back to his vehicle. All that time on the treadmill meant he'd hardly break a sweat.

The VW was noisy; the shifter felt like a twig, and it smelt funny. He would have preferred a less noticeable car, but beggars can't be choosers. If anyone came to the house, he'd make a run for it through the paddocks. He knew in advance which way to head and where to hide.

The coppers would soon work out who owned the car and be crawling all over Craig's folks' place and then Craig. It was tempting to make the call and see how it played out, but that would be stupid. He was a lot of things, but not stupid, unlike Craig.

One night in the change rooms, he'd overheard Craig offering the vehicle to a friend. The garage key was in the down pipe. The car keys under the front seat. The fool even said the address, his folks' place. No one was there over winter. People were stupid. Posting online while their homes were empty. Blurting out their address without knowing who's listening. But what piqued his interest was the way Craig described his father's garage.

The first time, he went just to have a look. Craig was interstate, and he wanted to see this garage. It was worth it. The way his old man had everything organised was impressive. An original VW Beetle sat under a car cover. Behind the wall was a home-brew set-up. It was then that he saw the barrels from Bennington Brewery.

That was where Sally Child worked. He couldn't even come and look at the garage without the wretched woman spoiling it. Later, when the urge came, the solution came to him. It was ingenious. He did the maths. The barrel was the right size. How perfect that someone who worked for a brewery would end up buried forever in one of their barrels. He'd taken the barrel and stored it in his garden shed.

He smiled at the memory. It had taken days to work out the details. How she would react when panic set in. Sally was fit. She would fight and kick, but she could never get out. Then all he had to do was wait for the right time.

He couldn't believe the answer had fallen into his lap so easily. He had come to recognise the good days versus the bad ones. The days when Olive's eyes were lucid and bright, and the whippet-smart brain was still visible. But it was on the bad days, when her eyes were glazed or staring off into the distance, that the gold came out. Like the details of Sally's date. At some point that night she would be alone. He just had to wait.

The road ahead was a long stretch of straight bitumen. On his left were paddocks with cows like statues. Enormous gum trees flanked either side of the road, their branches hanging precariously across the road.

He knew a woman up north whose daughter had died when a random tree struck her car as she drove home. The story stayed with him, and ever since then he kept one eye on the trees, his foot ready to speed up if there was any sign that a branch might topple on top of him.

He turned right faster than he meant to and veered onto the left side of the road. Gravel crunched underneath. With any luck, it hadn't damaged the paint. It was too late now, but he'd check when he arrived. The over-steering caused a clunking sound from the boot. The shovels. He'd done his research and landed on a twelve-gauge round-point shovel with a long fibreglass handle. He paid cash and bought two, so he had a backup. The soil in this part of the world was a dark reddish-brown clay with a strong fine crumb structure. It was highly suitable for berry crops and orchards, and, hopefully, tonight for burying a body.

He slowed. The entrance to the property was coming up. He recognised the burgundy-coloured milk can mailbox and turned right onto the track. The centre of the track had eroded, causing the VW to loll to one side. A loud clunk as the rear hit the dirt caused him to slow even further. He would have a hard time explaining things if he got stuck.

The quaint country house finally came into view. As expected, there were no lights on or sign anyone was home. The next tenants, with their fancy bottles of wine and antipasto snacks, weren't due until the following weekend, oblivious that Sally Child was buried nearby. If they knew, they would dine off the story for decades, but they would never find out. He'd make sure of that.

He smiled. These sheep never saw the wolf among them. Ivan Milat, Australia's worst serial killer, was described by his neighbour as a normal, friendly guy with a nice house and a tidy lawn. Not someone you felt uncomfortable or creeped out by. Unless you were on the end of the shotgun he had pointed straight at you.

What would they say about him? Polite and aloof. Likes to keep things to himself. If only they knew. Despite the internal turmoil he felt most days, he was good at keeping up appearances. He'd never felt the need for tattoos or weird haircuts or piercings. He wasn't after notoriety. The opposite, in fact. It was like keeping the exterior as normal as possible afforded him greater protection and privacy. Nor was he sensation-seeking. What he craved was to feel in control. As he got older, it had become more than a craving; he needed it.

Cutting the engine, he climbed out. The silence of the country calmed him. Using the light from his phone, he inspected the left bumper. The paint underneath was intact. Good. He didn't want Craig suspecting the car had been stolen. Who knew where that would lead? Itching to get started, he had to wait until the winery up the road closed.

Country rentals were dotted all around the hills. What if some drunk idiot called in by mistake, thinking it was their accommodation for the night. He would rest. Enjoy the quiet. He was going to need the energy.

44

Audrey drove along the bitumen road with Donna next to her, directing. There were no street lamps, so the only light came from the car's headlights and the reflector lights on posts at the entrance to each property. Trees lining both sides of the road blocked the view of homes that were set well back. During the weekend, the roads were busy with traffic visiting local wineries, but at night it was the opposite. The road was deserted, inky black, and eerie.

"This is it, on the right," said Donna.

Audrey slowed, and three hundred metres later a burgundy-coloured milk can mailbox was visible. Audrey turned into the driveway and stopped. "I want to try Cath again."

Audrey had left an earlier message letting Cath know what she had found on Alan Taylor and that he may be using a rental property in Red Hill, and had given her the address. Someone needed to know they were here. Cath deserved downtime like everyone, but it wasn't like her not to answer.

"Cath. It's Audrey, again. We're at the property now. We're not going to do anything. Just see if it looks like anyone's been here and then leave. But call me back."

She looked over at Donna. "You okay?"

Donna nodded, but some of her normal bravado was gone.

As they descended the track, the car rolled left and right where the earth had been washed away.

"I'd hate to come down here in the winter."

Audrey drove slowly so they didn't get bogged.

Donna was following the GPS. "The house isn't far. Maybe four hundred metres over that hill."

Audrey drove for another hundred metres, then pulled into a flat area and turned the lights off.

"Let's do the next bit on foot. If he's here, we don't want to alert him."

Alan Taylor was violent, and they had to be careful.

They climbed out.

Donna's face scrunched up. "What's that smell?"

"Chicken farm, I think. Make sure your phone is on silent."

Donna quickly followed the instruction. She must be nervous.

Using the lights from their mobile phones, they made their way along the track until the weatherboard cottage came into view.

The car wasn't there.

"Doesn't look like he's here."

Audrey didn't know whether to feel disappointed or relieved. "Let's look inside first. Keep the light on your phone down and turn it to silent. He could still turn up."

They made their way towards the front door and stepped onto the timber porch. Audrey tried the handle and was surprised to find it unlocked. She hesitated - why would it be open - then stepped into the hallway. On either side were bedrooms made up with warm, country furnishings. Audrey walked into the room on the right, Donna the one to the left. They met back in the hallway.

"Clear," Donna whispered. "I've always wanted to say that."

Farther down the hallway, Audrey pushed open the door to the bathroom. Nothing in there either. She followed Donna into a large open area with a kitchen at one end and a fireplace and sofas at the other.

Alan Taylor wasn't there, but neither was Sally. It was so disappointing.

Donna stood at the fireplace, then sat in one of the comfy-looking sofas that during the day would have a stunning view over the hills.

"This is a nice place."

"Agree."

It wasn't hard to imagine renters enjoying nights around it in one of Melbourne's freezing winters.

Audrey walked to the sink in the kitchen. The yard sloped away at the rear. To the right was a gravel path leading to the shed. Something caught her eye, beyond the path. She gasped and gripped the kitchen bench.

Metres to the right, in the darkness, with its bonnet open, was the VW.

Was Alan Taylor here?

Lowering her voice, she said, "Donna! Come here."

Donna hurried next to Audrey. It took a few seconds for her to register the car.

"What do we do? What if Sally is in there?"

Audrey's heart thudded. They should leave and ring the police. But tell them what? That Sally Child might be in a shed in Red Hill and to send someone? How long would that take?

"Is that a shovel?"

Audrey scanned the area and spotted the shovel against the side of the shed. If Alan Taylor had Sally in that shed and something happened to her… Leaving was no longer an option.

She hurried to the window facing the north side of the property. The ground sloped away quickly from the fence. They could make their way to the rear of the shed without being seen.

"Audrey. Audrey." There was an urgency in Donna's voice that made her hurry back to the sink.

Alan Taylor was walking towards the house.

Audrey grabbed Donna's arm and led her towards the front door. She had no desire to be stuck inside a house with a violent man. Once outside, she used the key to close it quietly behind them.

They were safer outside. But with no idea which direction he could come from, she gestured for Donna to wait. Several agonising seconds passed before the back door closed.

He was inside and walking up the hallway.

They could start running to the car, but if he came out the front door, he'd see them. Then what?

"Follow me."

Audrey hurried to the fence on the right side of the property. The wire fence pushed down easily. Once Donna was over, she led them down the paddock. The house was visible above and to their left, but she was confident they couldn't be seen.

There was no way to tell how long Alan would be inside, but this might be their only opportunity to look in the shed.

They continued right until the top of the shed came into view. There was no coverage along the next section of fence. Did they make a run for it and hope Alan wasn't watching? They had a better chance of not being seen if only one of them went.

"I'll go and look in the shed. If he comes out, call the police, and then come and help me."

Eyes bright, Donna nodded. "You sure?"

No.

Audrey made her way towards the shed.

45

Alan poured the sachet of minerals to give him energy into a glass of water and waited for it to dissolve. From here, he could make out the outline of the shed. The barrel had tucked nicely into the back corner.

A normal scream could travel five hundred metres, but between the barrel and the slope of the land, no one would hear, no matter how hard a person yelled. He'd already tapped the side, but as expected, there was no sign of life. The body can go without water for three, maybe four days, but not five.

Inside the barrel, the body would be cold, her limbs frozen stiff against the sides. Would her eyes and mouth be open or shut? It was tempting to remove the lid and see. Her skin would have a ghostly sheen, but he preferred to imagine this rather than smell the sour grape smell of death she would emit by now.

As the minerals dissolved, tiny bubbles and sparks aligned within him. It was like he'd been plugged into a power source he didn't understand. His pulse raced, and exhales shuddered with anticipation like a runner at the starting line. He tried to think of another time he'd felt so on it and in control but couldn't. Part of him didn't want it to end. Forever, he could think of Sally buried in a barrel tomb, but then what? His annoying colleague at work came to mind. Rhonda, or was it Rita? Another woman who wouldn't take the hint. The kernel of an idea formed. The urge stirred like a monster sitting at the bottom of his belly. Would he go again?

It was time. He chugged the drink in one, rinsed the glass, and placed it back on the shelf. After a final check to make sure he'd left no trace, he closed the back door and stepped out into the night air.

Inside the bonnet were gloves and a foldable hand trolley. He put on the gloves and unfolded the trolley. The gravel crunched underneath, and the earth squelched as he wheeled it across the grass. The rain had softened the earth. Good. Moisture would make it easier to dig.

The shed door squealed open. He wheeled the trolley in. Manoeuvring it into position, he tilted the barrel and slid it onto the footplate, then wheeled it outside. Returning to the shed, he moved a couple of items back into the corner and after a final check closed the door.

Walking backwards, he wheeled the trolley and barrel across the lawn towards a section of scrub at the bottom of the garden. He'd chosen the spot because it was so well hidden. Even someone mowing the lawns wouldn't venture into the thick scrub. The thought of Sally out here all alone would bring him joy for years. Sally Child would be the gift that kept on giving. And even if one day they miraculously found her body, there was no way to trace it back to him.

It wasn't the weight so much as having to push it across the soggy earth that was causing him to sweat. His arms ached as he pushed, and he could feel the strain across his back as he kept the trolley moving. With each step, the trolley seemed to sink further into the sodden earth, making it difficult for him to keep a steady pace. He arrived at the spot and, using the bottom of his T-shirt, wiped his forehead, then face and neck. The cool air against his warm skin caused it to tingle. Leaving the barrel on the trolley, he walked back to the shed and collected both shovels.

Marching down the grass with a shovel in each hand, he breathed in the night air. Oh, how he wanted to roar into the blackness and put a voice to how powerful he felt. Instead, he breathed in and filled his lungs with oxygen.

Holding one of the shovels, he walked to the middle of the scrub. Putting all his energy into it, the shovel sliced easily into the earth. It reminded him of the first time he had used a global knife to cut a cabbage. This wouldn't take long.

Careful to keep the soil and bush as intact as possible, he carefully placed each slice to the side, the loose dirt vanishing into the soil beneath. The shovel sliced into the earth again and again with ease. A bead of sweat rolled down his face, but instead of stopping to wipe it off, he let it finish its course, not wanting to interrupt the flow.

Instead of feeling tired from the task at hand, he felt strong and invigorated. If anything, his movements sped up. His skin burned and his muscles ached, yet he felt no pain, only an exhilaration pushing him forward.

46

T hat was lucky. Another moment and he would have seen her.
Audrey's heart raced as she listened to the sound of digging somewhere down the bottom of the yard. The shovel made a rhythmic thumping sound as it tore through the earth.

Audrey whispered, "He's burying something."

Or someone.

Despite the urge to confront Taylor to see what was in that barrel, they were two women alone with a potentially dangerous man.

Audrey's phone lit up.

Cath.

Finally.

She whispered into the phone. "Cath."

In the background were people talking and laughing. She was at a restaurant.

"Sorry. It's Michael's birthday dinner. He made me hand over my phone. Listen, I got your message. Do not go anywhere near this guy. Queensland police said a woman put a restraining order on him, and he's still the lead suspect in an attack on another woman, but they could never pin anything on him."

It was a bit late for that now.

Audrey whispered, "He's taken a barrel to the bottom of the garden and is digging a hole to bury something or someone."

"Shit. Hang on." Cath mumbled something, then came back on the line.

"I'm in Dromana. Be there in ten. Do not do anything until I get there." Cath didn't wait for a response and hung up.

"What did she say?"

"She's on her way."

Ten minutes was a long time. The thought of telling Olive and Bill they almost stopped him from hurting their daughter was too awful to consider. If Sally was in that barrel and alive, Audrey would never forgive herself.

She had to know.

"We need to see what he's burying, and we're going to need a weapon." Hopefully, there was something they could use in the shed. "Come on."

Audrey climbed over the wire fence, followed by Donna. They ran across the lawn to the shed. Audrey carefully opened the door, praying it didn't creak.

It didn't.

Donna held the door open while she looked for something to use. Two coffee tables stacked on top of one another, a lawn mower, and other eclectic items. In the corner was a plastic rake. It was useless, but behind it was a metal one and a digging fork. They would have to do. She spotted a ball of twine and grabbed it.

Outside she held up the rake and fork. "Any preference?"

Donna took the fork. "I used to do archery."

Another thing she didn't know about her colleague.

"Hopefully we won't have to use either, but it might buy us a few minutes until Cath gets here. Come on."

They stepped away from the shed and the coverage it provided and followed the trolley's imprint towards Alan and the digging sound.

Crunch. Groan. Crunch. Groan.

They couldn't see him, but the sound of the shovel slicing the earth, interspersed with his groans, appeared to be coming from behind a clump of shrubs in front of them.

To their right on the trolley was the barrel.

The digging slowed. Was the hole deep enough?

Audrey checked the time. Cath Maguire was a few minutes away.

There was no point in negotiating with a murderer. The only advantage they had was the element of surprise.

Eyes wide, Audrey handed Donna the twine.

"I'll hit him with the shovel. You tie his hands."

"What if I can't?"

It wasn't like Donna to sound unsure, and Audrey was momentarily rattled. She grabbed her arm. "Yes, you can."

The digging stopped.

It was time.

"Now!"

There was no turning back.

Audrey ran behind the scrub. Alan was in the hole and turned to see what the noise was. Eyes wide, at first he didn't realise what was happening, but then slowly he registered what was going on. He went to swing the shovel, but it caught on the earth.

Audrey took the opportunity to whack him in the back with the blunt side of the rake. He fell to his knees. Donna jumped in the hole and wrapped the twine around his arms while Audrey tried to grab his shovel. He managed to get one arm free and, grabbing Audrey's leg, knocked her backward onto the ground.

Sensing Audrey down, Alan used his free arm to punch her in the ribs. The pain was so intense, for several seconds she couldn't move. He was coming for her again when his arm dropped, and a wild scream echoed out into the night.

Donna had skewered his calf with the fork. "Move and I'll pull it out."

Audrey leapt into action and removed the shovel. Spitting and cursing, Alan tried to stand, but the pain was too great. His arm reached for the rake to remove it and then Donna, but she deftly managed to keep out of his way.

"I'll push it in farther."

Audrey held the shovel, ready to swing.

A car roared up the driveway.

Eyes wild, Alan gave Audrey a look that chilled her, and in that moment, there was little doubt about what this man was capable of.

47

Audrey was so relieved to see Cath Maguire marching down the grass towards her, she wanted to hug her. But then she saw Cath's expression. It was clear she wasn't pleased with Audrey or the fact that Donna had somehow managed to get a fork stuck in Alan's leg.

"I thought I told you to wait."

That was fair. Cath had to leave her husband's birthday dinner, and Audrey had ignored her instruction. Nevertheless, she felt the need to defend her actions.

"He had finished digging and was about to move the barrel. If anything happened because we stood by and waited…"

Alan spun his head and glimpsed at Cath in civilian clothes.

"Who the hell are you? What is this, Charlie's Angels?"

Cath leaned down so Alan could see her face and badge.

"Detective Cath Maguire to you."

His face fell.

Two officers came rushing down the property towards Cath.

Cath instructed the younger of the two to cuff him. And to the other, "You help me get this barrel open."

The officer looked around for something to pry the barrel open and spotted the fork in Alan's leg. Without hesitating, Donna pulled it out, causing Alan to scream in pain. There was no apology from Donna. One of the officers cuffed Alan, who groaned, and both men helped him out of the hole. He was livid. Was he being denied the part he'd been looking forward to the most — burying Sally Child? Audrey desperately hoped that wasn't the case, for Olive and Bill's sake, but it looked like it was.

As Alan was led up the lawn towards the police car, the remaining officer put on gloves and, taking the fork, tried to pry the top of the barrel. It wasn't the right instrument.

"I'm going to need a hammer and chisel."

"There might be one in the shed," said Donna. "I'll come with you."

They both headed up the lawn towards the shed.

Once they were out of earshot, Cath turned to Audrey.

"What the hell, Audrey!"

Audrey let Cath vent her frustration properly.

"One of these days, you're going to go too far."

It was hard to tell if her concern was as a friend or a police officer, likely a combination of both.

Donna and the officer returned with a hammer and a chisel that looked like it had seen better days. It was a slow process, but finally the top of the barrel came loose. The officer tapped each of the staves to loosen them from the lid.

The officer looked at Cath. "Do you want me to take it off?"

Cath nodded. "Go ahead."

Cath and Audrey stepped forward as the lid came off and they looked in the barrel.

Audrey's heart sank.

Inside was the top of a woman's head. She recognised the light brown silky hair from the photos. They had found Sally Child, but it was too late. It was crushing.

A brief respectful silence settled over the site, but then it was time to get to work. Audrey and Donna moved back as Cath called the medical examiner.

"Thanks, Evelyn. See you soon."

Cath said something to the officer, who headed back to the car and walked over.

"You two have had quite a night. I suppose I should be grateful."

There was little victory in finding Sally.

Cath looked at Donna.

Audrey did the introductions.

"This is Donna. She's a colleague at the paper. She's training to be a journalist."

"Under you?"

"Ha-ha." The attempted humour did nothing to lighten the bleakness of the scene.

Cath's eyes widened. "How about you both run me through what happened while we wait for the ME."

Audrey filled Cath in on Cara and Alan, Craig's missing car, and any relevant details she could think of while Donna chimed in with the details she missed.

Twenty minutes later, a woman in her late forties in work boots, chinos, and a quilted jacket strode towards them, followed by two investigators. Evelyn had a round, rosy face and a shock of shoulder-length black curly hair that reminded Audrey of a sheep.

"Ladies."

Cath patted Audrey's arm before walking over to join her. It was her way of saying she'd done well, but Olive and Bill's daughter was dead. No matter which way you looked at it, the ending was anything but a success.

Evelyn and her colleagues inspected the body. Audrey had no desire to see Sally removed from the barrel and gestured to Donna. It was time to go.

"You're kidding me." Cath's head recoiled.

Audrey stopped. Something was going on. The others sensed it as well, and all eyes were now on Evelyn.

"We've got a pulse, people."

Audrey couldn't believe it.

The race was now on to save Sally Child's life.

Cath called an ambulance. The nearest station was Rosebud, ten minutes away at normal speed. Six or seven if they left straight away and sped.

Under Evelyn's guidance, the team carefully removed the barrel encasing Sally. Arms linked, Audrey and Donna stood frozen. Audrey didn't want to watch, but nor could she leave.

An ambulance siren roared up the driveway, and two paramedics rushed down the lawn. After what felt like an eternity, Sally's limp body was placed onto a stretcher. Outwardly, there was no sign of life. As Sally was taken away, Audrey prayed that whatever faint pulse had kept her alive until now could hang in there a bit longer.

48

Bennington Hospital was the major hospital on the Mornington Peninsula. As Audrey and Donna walked towards Sally's room, Audrey felt a mix of excitement and pure joy. They had saved a woman's life. Donna looked over, grinning. These were the days that made it all worthwhile. No words were necessary.

They arrived at Sally's room. "This is it."

"Let's do this," said Donna.

Sally was sitting up in bed, looking pale and exhausted but very much alive. Her knuckles were bandaged, no doubt damaged from trying to escape the prison she found herself in. Olive was tidying her bedside table while Bill and Rick were watching workmen working on yet another extension to the already sprawling building. It was almost a shame to disturb the peaceful family scene, but Audrey had questions she hoped Sally was up to answering.

Audrey knocked gently and stepped inside. Sally looked over, momentarily confused, which was understandable, since they had never met. Olive didn't recognise them either and turned to Bill. "Are these the ladies?"

Bill smiled. "Yes, they are."

He took Audrey's hands in both of his, then repeated the gesture with Donna. "We can't thank you both enough."

Audrey was about to say how pleased she was that things turned out the way they did when Olive suddenly wrapped her arms around her. Audrey's family weren't big huggers, but rather than flinching, she leaned into the warmth of the experience, sniffing to keep her composure.

Olive kissed her on the cheek. "Thank you."

It was now Donna's turn. She seemed more at ease with having Olive's arm wrapped around her.

Rick was next. "Yeah, like Mum said, thanks for helping to get Sal back to us." He gave both women awkward hugs, then stepped back.

With that over, Audrey was keen to speak to Sally alone. "It's nice to meet you, Sally. I wish it was under different circumstances."

"Me too."

Sally had a pleasant voice. Modulated. Comforting. The kind of voice that made you feel like everything would be okay. It was nice to hear her speak. But Audrey's questions were not necessarily ones she could ask around the others.

She directed her question to Bill. "Do you mind if I have a few minutes alone with Sally?"

Bill hesitated and looked at Sally. "I'm fine, Dad."

"How about I shout us all coffee at the canteen?" said Donna. Their divide-and-conquer strategy worked well.

Olive's eyes lit up. "I like a cappuccino with chocolate on top."

"Fine with me," said Rick.

The others filed out of the room, and Sally slumped back on the pillow. "I can't believe it was Alan. I knew he wasn't interested in anything romantic, but I thought we were friends."

It was going to take a while to process that someone she knew tried to kill her. "That must have been a shock to find out. Was he the one who approached you in your car?"

Sally nodded. "A lot of things are hazy, but I remembered being with him in the park at the end of the Main Street."

There were plenty of approved drugs that caused people to lose their memory. Some were used in the treatment of moderate to Alzheimer's disease and came as a pill or syrup. Alan worked in aged care, so it wouldn't be difficult to know what ones to use.

"Did you go out for a drink?"

Sally shook her head. "I don't remember."

It had only been two days. Hopefully with time Sally would remember the details, but regardless, Alan Taylor was guilty. With his violent past and finding him with Sally's body, he would be locked away for a long time.

"Do you have any idea why he targeted you?"

"No." Sally looked down. "I know I can be full-on at times, but after he said he wasn't interested, I thought there's no reason we can't be friends, so I still spoke to him."

She breathed deep to quell the panic.

Audrey waited until she was calm again. "Alan has a history of being violent towards women. People who take pleasure from humiliating, scaring, or other forms of harm to a person may crave a feeling of power because they normally feel powerless in day-to-day life."

Sally looked genuinely bewildered. "But he runs his own business and doesn't have a partner or any kids. How could someone like that feel powerless?"

Experts would spend years of taxpayers' money working with Alan to unlock exactly that. Audrey couldn't help wondering whether the answer lay in his early life in the Boroughs.

"Who knows what goes on in a mind like that?"

There was the matter of the USB and who was at Sally's house that night. Cath's team had found the USB and was reviewing its contents.

"I want to ask a couple of questions about work."

Sally flinched.

Audrey had to tread carefully. "Your parents and friends said you used to talk about work a lot, but then stopped. Was there anything going on at work before you went missing?"

Sally wrung her hands. "I'm not sure I should speak to you about that."

Audrey felt bad pushing Sally but pressed on. "We know you kept a USB with sensitive information. The police found it when they searched your house."

Cath's team had missed it the first time but found it on the second visit. The details weren't important.

Sally looked out the window, processing that this now meant the end of her job and possible convictions for Lucas and Trish, and so Audrey gave her a minute before continuing.

"We believe someone went looking in your home for the USB while you were missing. Any idea who that might be?"

Sally's eyes darted around. "The only people who know the code to my place are my parents. Not even Rick knows it because of his last girlfriend."

"How about Gavin?"

"Gav. No. He doesn't have it either."

"Is there any chance your mum could have told him or anyone else the code?"

"I don't think so, but I'm not sure of anything anymore."

Sally put her head back on the pillow. She was tired.

"Some of your customers mentioned you weren't happy with a few things at work. That type of information has a way of getting back to employers. Is there any way they could have known you had confidential information on the business? Maybe checked whether any files had been opened?"

Sally frowned. "Everyone grumbles about work sometimes, but I love my job."

"So there's no chance someone saw you copying the information?"

Sally shook her head adamantly.

It was time to circle back to Gavin. "I wanted to ask you a few questions about Gavin."

Sally seemed surprised. "Gav?"

Audrey smiled, trying to keep it light. "Has he been in to see you?"

"Not yet," said Sally, registering that her best friend hadn't been in. "I'm sure he will today."

Maybe.

"I know you work together. Is there any chance he knew you had information on the business?"

Sally shook her head. "Gav gets worried too easily, so I never told him what I found. I didn't want him having to lie for me in case anyone found out."

If someone suspected Sally had been copying company information, going via Gavin, her best friend, was one way to find out. Perhaps even offer him something in return.

"Gavin likes his job, doesn't he?"

Going by his social media, the brewery, Sally, and her family were the main things in his life.

"He loves it."

"Let's say that your employers, Lucas and Trish, found certain files had been opened and potentially copied. They ask Gavin, who denies knowing anything because it's the truth."

Audrey let Sally consider this before continuing. "But what if they threatened his job if he didn't find the information?"

Sally frowned. "He would have told me."

"But what if they said not to? In fact, they said if he did say anything to you, he would lose his job."

Sally was less sure this time. "I mean, I'd like to think he would tell me, but I suppose there's a chance he might not if his job was at stake."

"Unless... Gav's whole life was the brewery and us. If he thought he'd lose both..." Sally's voice trailed off.

Audrey leaned in. "I know this is hard, but did you ever notice Gavin doing anything unusual at your house? Looking at your computer. In the shed. Was he in a room he normally wouldn't be in?"

Sally shook her head but then froze, like she was remembering something. She averted her eyes out the window to buy time. Perhaps tying information together? Audrey waited, praying there was a queue at the canteen and the others wouldn't arrive back yet. Her phone buzzed. Donna. *On our way.*

Sally finally spoke. "One night he picked me up as we were going to a friend's birthday. He was early, which was odd, as Gav's always a bit late. He asked if he could make a cuppa while I finished getting ready, but when I came out, he was in the kitchen looking in the drawers. He said he was looking for tea bags. I don't know anyone who keeps tea bags in their kitchen drawers."

Neither did Audrey.

"He made a joke about it and said he didn't feel like one anymore. It's probably nothing, right?"

Audrey didn't believe that. Nor did Sally, judging by the colour in her cheeks. "He'd come and tell me. I know he would."

Audrey wasn't so sure. The police would need to speak to him and find out. It might also explain why he ran from her.

Audrey checked her notes. The word *will* was circled. "Gavin seems to be close to your parents."

"Yes. His own aren't around, so they've kind of adopted him as another son. Rick gets a bit jealous, but he gets it. Gav's good to them and helps them out a fair bit."

"Do you think Gavin expected to be a beneficiary of their will? As a reward for the support he provided?"

Sally recoiled. "I don't think so. Why would he?"

"Why would he do what?" Olive said, walking back in with the others. A tiny drop of foam sat on her top lip.

Donna gave Audrey an apologetic look. She'd tried to keep them away as long as possible.

Sally continued. "Whether Gav expected to be a beneficiary in your will."

"Why on earth would he think that?" Bill looked confused.

But Olive was quiet.

Sally watched her mother. "Mum. Did you say anything to him?"

"I might have told him there'd be a little something for him when we pass."

Bill's back arched. "Why would you say that Olive?"

Olive looked chastened.

"Mum. Why did you say that?" Rick's tone was kinder, but he was still annoyed.

"I felt sorry for him, but then we redid the wills, and your father wanted to leave your shares to Monash, and so that was the end of that. I didn't want him turning up expecting money, so I told him about the change."

"What did he say?" Sally looked worried.

"He seemed hurt. Not about the money, but I think he thinks he's part of our family."

Gavin had put his affection out there for Sally and had it denied and now had the promise of being legally acknowledged as part of a family taken away.

The car. If Alan Taylor knew about the VW in Craig's garage, Gavin would have known about it. Had he also borrowed Craig's car to visit Sally's that night? Maybe even Trish or Lucas suggested the idea? If anyone noticed a car outside Sally's, they would look at Craig first.

Audrey looked at Sally. "Knowing that, and how much that might have hurt him, is there any chance Gavin would have helped them?"

As Sally's face crumbled at the betrayal, Audrey wondered if her theory was right, and Lucas and Trish had managed to get Gavin to betray his best friend.

49

Armani's restaurant was busy. Audrey couldn't help wondering whether the waiter now taking their order was the one who had served Sally and her date the previous week. It didn't matter. Sally was alive, and Leon Reeves was an innocent man.

"I wonder which table she sat at," said Beth, scanning the other tables filled with patrons.

It wasn't like Beth to show much interest in Audrey's work, so when she had suggested coming to the place where Sally's night began, Audrey didn't object. There was no way she would have agreed if Sally hadn't survived, but it seemed harmless, and the place had good reviews.

Mark picked up his drink. "Let's raise a toast to Mum for helping to catch the bad guy."

Helping. She had done more than that, but he would lose his mind if he knew Audrey and Donna had approached someone so dangerous with only a fork and rake. All she told him was that they had managed to track Alan's car to the rental property and that the police then came and arrested him.

She did tell him she was there when they discovered Sally Child inside the barrel. It was going to take a while to forget the image of Sally being pried from the barrel, if ever. In the short term, it would haunt her dreams and perhaps even cause a nightmare or two. He was her husband and needed to know. But time was a great healer, so longer-term she hoped, like all the other bad memories, it would fade.

Josh picked up his Coke. "Good work, Mum."

Audrey smiled. "Thank you."

Beth raised her lemonade. "Congratulations."

Audrey sensed a "but" coming.

"Pity you weren't there when they opened the barrel and found her."

Mark cast her a secret glance. She was glad she had told him, but they decided not to tell the kids. Beth's questions would be relentless, and Audrey had no desire to continue to relive the harrowing experience as new ones came to mind.

"Oh, well."

Underneath the table, Mark's leg brushed hers. It felt nice. These were the best days. The ones when they were used to each other again, and the world felt back in balance.

Josh turned to his father. "Dad, can we go to the Quay tomorrow? I want to check out this new hoodie I've got my eye on."

Mark smiled. "Don't see why not."

Josh grinned. He was a teenage boy and loved having his father around. Beth had a strange expression on her face. Was she put out and wanted to go? Soon Mark would go back to his life on the rig, and once again Audrey would be the sole parent. The kids would eat meals with one parent. Time with their father was special for Beth as well.

"I've got an idea."

She fully expected it to crash and burn but continued. "Why don't we all go to the Quay tomorrow? You boys can check out hoodies, and Beth can take me shopping. Might be time to get a new outfit, and then we can go and have lunch somewhere?"

Mark winked at Audrey. They should be so lucky that their daughter was even considering an outing with her parents.

Beth picked up her phone. "That might work."

"Hey, can we get sushi for lunch?" Josh asked.

"Works for me," said Audrey.

Beth showed her phone to Mark. Was she picking out new clothes for Audrey already? Whatever it was, Mark seemed to approve.

"Can I see?"

Beth showed Audrey her screen. It was a pair of chinos and a white cream blouse. Nice. "I thought we could start with some things for work."

Audrey took a deep breath and looked at Mark. "Should be fun."

Outside, Cath Maguire walked past with a female colleague, carrying takeaway. They looked happy and upbeat.

"Back in a sec."

Audrey hurried outside. "Cath!"

Cath spotted her and smiled. She turned to her colleague. "Be there in a minute." Turning back to Audrey, she said, "Night out on the town?"

Audrey smiled too. "With the family, at least. Mark and the kids are inside. Long night ahead?"

Cath shrugged. "You know. Crime never sleeps."

Audrey waited until Cath's colleague was in the car and the door closed. "Another trainee detective?"

Cath sighed. "I keep telling these recruits that it's not like being a normal copper where you go home and come back the next day to a new slate of calls. We get assigned a case and work it until they're solved, or we reach a dead end, but I think some of them miss the uniform and sirens, you know."

Before she could think about it, Audrey blurted out, "Do you love your job?"

Cath stopped. Anyone else might think this was a bizarre question to ask right now, but not Cath. "Sure, the hours suck sometimes, but yes, I love it. Nothing I'd rather be doing."

Audrey felt an odd pang of jealousy. "We should grab a bite to eat one night. Just the two of us."

"Sure. I'd like that. Text me a couple of nights that work. Better go. Our dumplings are getting cold."

Audrey watched Cath hop back into her car. Was she jealous of her old school friend solving crimes day and night? Australia wasn't like the UK, where you could go straight into a junior detective role and climb the ranks from there. It took years in the police force before being considered for detective training. Audrey had no desire to be a patrol officer or a private investigator either.

So if she didn't want to be a detective, why the sudden jealousy of Cath? She had witnessed the camaraderie between prosecutors and judges with the detectives she dealt with on a regular basis. But she had that with Donna and Stan, albeit in a more modest way. She had been at crime scenes where people directed their questions to the detective over the officers with badges. Was it respect and acknowledgement she craved? That felt a little closer, but she didn't crave public adulation like Cam Andrews. Aro Chol's case had taught her that.

Jack's case had given her the opportunity to uncover council corruption, Aro Chol how we treat those different from us, and Sally Child how they had a long way to go before females felt safe. But then the demands of filling the daily news prevented her from writing the bigger, more important stories beyond what happened to them. The ones she became a journalist to write. The ones that took weeks or even months to complete but then impacted countless lives. Was it time to take things up a notch?

Back at the table, Mark looked at her. "Everything okay?"

She smiled. "No, but it will be."

50

Audrey waited at the start of Bennington pier for Sally. The place held so many memories. Not all of them were good, but it was a pleasant change from the typical catch-up in a coffee shop.

It had been two weeks since Sally left the hospital, and walking towards her, she looked physically stronger. Her face had regained its colour, and her strides were purposeful. Her posture was straight, and her arms moved with strength. The bandages on Sally's hands were gone, but the internal scars would take much longer to heal.

Charges had been laid against the owners of the brewery and the business put into liquidation until further notice. Gavin confessed to breaking into Sally's, stating they gave him no choice if he wanted to keep his job. Lucas was the one who told him about the VW sitting in Craig's parents' garage after overhearing Craig at the gym. Gavin's willingness to help the investigation would reduce whatever penalty he faced, but the betrayal was too much for Sally. Their friendship was over.

"Morning." She sounded upbeat and gave Audrey a peck on the cheek. "It feels good to be back exercising."

"I'll bet."

A wave broke near them. They both hurried to higher ground, straining their legs to get out of the way of the water. Audrey looked back to see the last bits of the wave slowly evaporate into the sand.

"I've got an interview today with one of my customers."

Sally's face glowed with enthusiasm. Was it Lixin?

"Good for you." Audrey waited for her to elaborate.

"He wants me to look at the entire operation and redo processes, plus some sales. Mum thinks it's too soon, but it's not good for me to do nothing. I start next week."

Raising her hands, she clapped them joyfully.

Audrey found solace in her work as well. The way her fingers moved over the keyboard, helping her focus on the words, caused her body to quiet and relax. Her mind still wandered, but the rhythm of her typing became her own form of meditation.

"Speaking of my folks, Mum and Dad asked if you'd like to come over for dinner and bring your family."

Audrey hadn't seen Olive and Bill since their visit to the hospital, and she was keen to catch up with them again. She did a mental review of the week's commitments. "That sounds terrific. We could do Wednesday night, if that works."

"Wednesday's good," said Sally.

Beth would be excited at the prospect of meeting Sally Child and dine off the experience with her friends for weeks, if not months. It wasn't often Audrey's work impressed her daughter, so that would be a nice side benefit. Josh would want to know what they were cooking for dinner. Mark was back on the rig and would miss out, which was a pity. He would have enjoyed meeting the woman who stole his wife's attention for the best part of the week.

They continued on a bit farther. Sally was grinning, and Audrey had the feeling there was something else.

"Leon called me."

Leon, who had been the primary suspect for the best part of a week. "How is he going?"

Sally smiled. "He said it was pretty stressful, but once they caught Taylor, everything settled down. He said, no rush, but he would like to catch up again when I'm ready."

"Are you going to see him again?"

Sally looked at her. "I wasn't sure at first, because for days I thought he was the one who put me in there, but now I know he wasn't, I think so."

If things worked out between them, it was a hell of a story to start their relationship. How easily it could have been a different ending.

A violent man had tried to kill Sally and nearly succeeded. She was one of the lucky ones who survived. Others wouldn't be so fortunate. It was a continuum of behaviours starting with seemingly harmless sexist jokes that further along the line were connected to behaviours that caused women and girls serious harm, disability, and even death. The best thing Audrey could do was continue writing about the issue and raise a kind, respectful son. Every bit helped.

A small speed boat drove past to their left. The vessel bobbed along the water with its captain at the wheel. More would appear as the morning wore on. Sally breathed in the morning air. Audrey could only imagine the horror of being stuck in a barrel with limited air. She would want to capture every bit of fresh air she could now as well.

Audrey was happy for the part she had played in ensuring Sally got to do that.

REVIEW & STAY IN TOUCH

I hope you enjoyed getting to know Audrey Lord and her colleagues as much as I enjoy writing them. Audrey can seem cool and aloof at times, but underneath she's driven by a deep hunger for truth and justice.

If you did enjoy the story, I'd be incredibly grateful if you left a review. Not only do I love hearing what readers think, but reviews help others discover my books and decide if they're right for them.

If you'd like to stay up to date with new releases or learn more about the Mornington Peninsula, where I live and where the series is set, you can sign up to my mailing list at gcchase.com.

They say authors often write themselves into their books, and I'm no exception. Like Audrey, I returned to the Peninsula after years interstate and overseas, and like her, I've learned to love it again. With its stunning beaches, more than 200 wineries, and pockets of native forest, the Peninsula is undeniably beautiful, but it's also shaped by distance, isolation, and a quiet, lingering restlessness.

In places like this, trouble, and sometimes murder, have a way of surfacing.

AUDREY LORD SERIES

If you haven't yet explored the other books in the series, I'd love for you to discover how Audrey's investigations began and follow her development across each case. While each book can be read as a standalone, together they build a deeper portrait of small-town Australia and the complex moral questions we all face.

And if you haven't already, don't forget to visit my website to claim your free novella. It tells the story of how it all started for Audrey, and offers a glimpse into the events that shaped her into the determined investigative journalist.

Thank you for your support, and happy reading!

Visit gcchase.com

THE PERMIT (Book 1)

He's dead. The police say suicide. She knows better.

Twenty years ago, Audrey Lord left Bennington behind — its beaches, its secrets, and Jack Masters, the boy she once loved.

Now Jack is dead. Officially? Suicide. But nothing about it makes sense.

Back on Victoria's Mornington Peninsula, juggling two kids and a job at the local paper, Audrey never planned to dig into the past. But Jack's father is convinced it was murder and Audrey owes Jack more than silence. She starts pulling at threads that lead to council corruption, shady land deals, and powerful people with everything to lose.

As Audrey and Leonard investigate, the pressure mounts. Her job is on the line. Her relationships are fracturing. And someone is watching her every move.

In a town where everyone has something to hide, the truth could get her killed.

THE STAIN (Book 2)

A dead teenager. An exclusive community. Was it really an accident?

When Sudanese-Australian student Aro Chol is found dead at the foot of the prestigious Chilton Hill estate, local journalist Audrey Lord is first on the scene. Residents claim he was trying to break in. The police suspect a fall. At police request, Audrey agrees to report it as an accident—for now.

But Aro was no criminal. He was a bright student with big dreams—not someone who'd throw his future away for a petty crime. Sneaking into one of the wealthiest, most tightly secured homes on the Mornington Peninsula doesn't add up.

As Audrey digs deeper, she uncovers a web of buried tensions among Chilton Hill's elite, within Aro's former community, and even inside his own family. With race tensions rising and public pressure mounting, everyone has something to hide and everyone wants to control the story.

She wants to give Aro's family answers. But if she's wrong, it could cost her career and leave a killer free to strike again.

THE VANISHED (Book 3)

People don't just vanish without a trace... or do they?

When Sally Child disappears after a night out with a mystery date, those closest to her know something's wrong. Some believe she left willingly—but her family, and local journalist Audrey Lord, aren't convinced. Sally was steady, reliable. She wouldn't walk away without a word.

As Audrey investigates, a different picture of Sally begins to emerge—tensions at work, cracks in her friendships, and secrets she kept even from those who knew her best. But the biggest questions remain: Who was her date? Why hasn't he come forward? And what was Sally hiding?

Missing persons cases don't stay in the headlines for long, and time is running out. Audrey is determined to find answers before Sally becomes another forgotten face. But when the investigation takes an unexpected turn, everything finally clicks into place. The only question now is: are they too late?

THE MILLERS (Book 4)

The granddaughter of the woman who made your life hell goes missing—then asks for your help. What do you do?

When journalist Audrey Lord is asked by her longtime nemesis, Sharon Miller, to help find her kidnapped granddaughter, she's stunned and deeply wary. Two decades ago, Sharon ran Audrey out of Bennington. Helping her now feels unthinkable.

But a child is missing, and the clock is ticking.

Most abductions involve someone close to home but the Millers have enemies. Plenty of them. Old feuds, buried secrets, and bitter rivalries mean the list of suspects is long. Even Audrey has a motive.

As she's pulled deeper into Sharon's murky world, Audrey doesn't know who to trust. Is Sharon a grieving grandmother or a master manipulator playing one last game?

Visit gcchase.com